THE PRINCESS AND THE PRINCIPAL

THE REBEL ROYALS BOOK 5

SHANAE JOHNSON

THOSE JOHNSON GIRLS

Copyright © 2020, Ines Johnson. All rights reserved.
This novel is a work of fiction. All characters, places, and incidents described in this publication are used fictitiously, or are entirely fictional. No part of this publication may be reproduced or transmitted, in any form or by any means, except by an authorized retailer, or with written permission of the author.

Edited by Alyssa Breck

Manufactured in the United States of America
First Edition April 2020

PROLOGUE

Molly Romano kicked the back of her Hush Puppies against the leg of the swivel chair. She'd chosen to sit in the grown-up chairs at the Principal's desk rather than at the small table with the bright orange and red chairs that had the cutouts in the back. She'd never understood why elementary school chairs had the cutouts in the backs? Did teachers think kids needed the ventilation at their backs and bottoms?

From her perch, she looked around the inner sanctum of the leader of her newest school. It was her fourth school in six years. That is if you count kindergarten. This would be her third principal's office visit in that time.

On the walls were, of course, pictures of the man

in charge surrounded by kids. Like all the other pictures on the other principals' walls, this one was dressed in a clean white shirt. He had graying hair, but a young face. A very young face. Just looking at his face, Molly would've guessed this man was her mom's age.

Another difference that this principal had over the other two was the kids around him. They were actually grinning, not smiling as though they were being forced. The kids looked like they were having a good time. A few of them were looking up at the principal as though they even liked him.

On the desk was also a gold placard that proudly displayed the words Principal. There was an emphasis on the end of the word as PAL in red, capital letters. Molly supposed it was to indicate that the man wanted to be friends with the kids.

There was also a picture of the same man dressed as Santa. Molly was old enough to know that Santa didn't exist. Her father had told her so when she was five despite her mother's protests. He did tell her that reindeer were real but didn't fly. Rabbits didn't lay eggs. There was also no Tooth Fairy.

He'd promised there were no monsters in her closet. But she wasn't so sure about that one. She was sure there hadn't been any in her old home which had been an apartment. On the other side of the closet had been her parents' bedroom. She'd heard them arguing loud enough to scare away any potential closet monsters.

She now lived in an old house. It looked like a small castle. Because it had been a castle. But that was over a hundred years ago when one of her grandfather's ancestors had built it as a summer castle. Though the rooms were small. Molly wasn't sure what was on the other side of her new closet. But it was quiet in her grandparents' old house. All so very quiet.

Molly hated it.

A knock sounded on the other side of the door. Molly wondered if she should say come in? But there was no need. The door swung open and in the frame stood the man that was in the picture frames.

He didn't bow at the waist. He didn't bow his head either. Many of Cordoba's citizens didn't practice the old ways in this new age. Unless it was with King Leonidas or Prince Alexandar. Definitely not with a distant cousin who wasn't close enough on the branches of the family tree to be given the title of princess.

"Good afternoon, Molly."

The principal's smile was big and bright. Molly was instantly suspicious. Instead of greeting him the way she was taught by her mother -with manners- she stared mutely; the way she'd observed her father do.

"My name is Principal Kidd."

He stuck out his hand. Molly was already in enough trouble, she decided to show she did have some manners. She shook his hand. But lightly, and not firmly like her grandpa had taught her.

"I hear you've been causing a bit of mischief in your class," Principal Kidd said as he took his seat.

Molly shrugged. "It was just a joke."

"Mrs. Steen didn't think so. She didn't think glitter on the whiteboard eraser was a laughing matter."

"I still say that it could've been a fairy come to brighten her dull lesson."

And that tall tale would've stuck. But the whole class had told on her. Every single head had turned to her, many fingers pointed, her name came out of the mouth of each kid in the classroom. What kind of kids didn't appreciate a joke played on the teacher? Especially a lemon-pinched mouth, something-smells-bad nosed, beady-eyes-peering-over glasses teacher like Mrs. Steen.

Since she'd been here the last two weeks, not a single person had missed a homework assignment. Every hand went up when the teacher asked a question. Molly was sure she was in the Upside Down version of schools and Mrs. Steen was a Demogorgon sucking the spirit out of these kids.

But the principal didn't try to abduct her into another realm. He leaned back in his own adult-sized swivel chair and chuckled softly. It wasn't a monstrous, big belly laugh. He didn't flash sharp teeth. It was almost a giggle, like when she and her mother used to have tickle wars.

"Mrs. Steen said that the other day you erased the numbers on her ruler?"

"We were talking about world leaders. I was trying to participate in the lesson with a utilitarian ruler."

Now the principal threw back his head and outright laughed. It surprised Molly. It had been so long since she'd heard an adult laugh, especially a man. Her father was always frowning, or upset, or just plain angry.

"You're a smart kid, Molly. You have a great imagination."

Molly couldn't figure this guy out? "So, you're

not going to suspend me? Or give me after school detention?"

The gray-haired man with the young man's face tilted his head like Tweety Bird. "Why would I do that?"

"Because what I did was… wrong."

Principal Kidd nodded.

Uh oh. Was this it? Had she slipped and fallen into his trap? Was he now going to tell her that she was doing what she did for attention? She'd watched a couple of episodes of the Dr. Phil show with her grandma. This was some of that reversal psychology.

"I've read your file," he said. "Before coming to Barton Elementary, you've been to three different schools in the past six years."

"My family moved around a lot."

"But you've always received high marks in your academics…and a lot of notes about your behavior."

Principal Kidd lifted his brow at her. But he didn't roll his eyes like the last two principals did. Or like her father did when she tried to talk to him but he was too busy, always too busy.

Principal Kidd didn't look too busy at all. He didn't frown or look upset, or angry. He was still smiling at her.

It reminded her of how her mom smiled. In fact, his laugh had also reminded Molly of her mom. It had been so long since she'd heard her mom laugh.

"I think you're a special kid," Principal Kidd was saying. "In fact, you're my favorite kind of kid; smarts and imagination. I think you can fit in here if you give us a chance."

Molly felt something twitch in her chest. She gazed up at the principal and the sincerity in his gaze. He wasn't playing any tricks. He meant it. Maybe he wasn't like the rest? Maybe she could give him a chance?

"I will have to call your parents."

And now she wanted to revoke that chance. Her shoulders slumped at the thought of her mother receiving yet another call from a school. "It's just my mom."

"I'm guessing by your tone, she won't think the fairy eraser was funny?"

"She would've thought so. Before the divorce. Now she's always so serious."

Instead of reaching for the phone, Principal Kidd leaned forward. "My parents are divorced too. They got divorced when I was your age."

Molly spied a picture at the corner of the principal's desk. In it was a picture of an even younger version of the man, still with gray hair. He wore a square cap on his head and was dressed in a dark cape. Likely his graduation. He was standing between two smiling adults.

"Yup, that's them. Oh, they get along. They just weren't right for each other. They're both happily remarried to other people."

Molly knew her dad was seeing other women. He'd started while he and her mom were still married. Maybe that's why they got divorced? Molly wasn't sure. But her dad did seem happier now. The few times she'd seen him since the divorce.

Her mom hadn't dated any other man at all. Maybe her mom should start to date? Then maybe she'd laugh again.

Just like the principal laughed...

Molly looked up at Principal Kidd. He didn't have a ring on his left hand. She hadn't seen any pictures of him with women his own age. Just pictures of him with his parents and with kids.

"What's your mom's name?" he asked. "Oh, I've got it here. Kylee..."

"Kylee Romano," Molly finished for him. "But she's going by her original name, her maiden name."

"Kylee Bauer? Your mom is Kylee Bauer?"

"Yes. Do you know her?"

"Yeah," said Principal Kidd. "Yeah, I know Princess Kylee Bauer."

Molly rarely heard her mom's name spoken with the royal title. It was as though most of the country had forgotten who she was after her father ran off to marry a commoner. But Molly supposed these were different times. After all, both King Leo and Prince Alex had married commoners. And Queen Esme and Princess Jan weren't even Cordovian. They were Americans.

But Principal Kidd wasn't looking as though he was disapproving of her family. His eyes got that gooey faraway look like a Looney Tunes cartoon character when they fell in love.

Wait? So, Principal Kidd knew her mom. And he got the lovey-dovey look just at hearing her name. And he wasn't married.

A plan began to form in Molly's brain. One that would require a bit of imagination and probably some fairy sparkles if it were to work.

CHAPTER ONE

"We can't keep going over this again and again."

Kylee Bauer looked up at the kid looming over her. He couldn't be more than twenty-two, fresh out of college, making more than she ever made in her twenty-nine years. But he was her supervisor.

He was also shorter than her, which was why she was sitting. She'd dealt with boys like him her whole life. Short, insecure, little lordlings who would take credit for the work she did because they were threatened by her intelligence.

But Kylee hadn't had the use of her title in years. Anthony Sims wouldn't know that he should bow to her rather than lord over her. It didn't matter because it was Kylee who wasn't on his level.

Anthony knew more about AI-generated learning programs than she did.

Just a decade ago, Kylee had been at the top of her high school classes. She'd earned a full scholarship partially based on her perfect SAT scores. She'd planned to major in Instructional Design. But that was all before she'd further disgraced her already disgraced family by getting pregnant in her sophomore year at university. She'd had to take a temporary leave from college that turned into two years.

By the time she'd managed to finish her degree a few years later, everything in the academic testing world had changed. Gone were the personalized curriculum planning and lesson plans she'd been introduced to in her freshman year. Now everything was digital, and Kylee was still stuck in an analog world.

With her Number 2 pencil in hand, she scratched out a circle on her notepad -the old fashion parchment, not a computer tablet. "I'm sorry, Anthony. Do you think you can explain the program to me one more time?"

The co-ed sighed. His head fell to his chin, giving Kylee a glimpse of the back of the man bun on top of his head.

"Actually, you know what," she said. "I think I've got it now."

Kylee tapped a few keys and prayed. Someone up above was listening because the program beeped to life and began to run. She tried to hide the surprise from her face as she looked back up at Anthony.

He eyed her skeptically. But luckily for her, he had a short attention span like many in this generation who spent their days staring at screens. Hardly anyone in the office of Thrive Learning Systems held a pencil. That was a shame because every standardized test from the SATs to the ACTs to the International Baccalaureate Exams all still required the use of pencil and paper.

Kylee looked back to the test she was in the midst of preparing a preparatory course for. Her problem remained that she had no clue how she'd gotten it to work. She still didn't fully understand the inner workings of the new system. What she did know was how to prepare lessons and assessments.

She pulled out the sharpener for her pencil. There was something satisfying in watching the shavings fall off the lead. The pencil was being born anew as well as getting sharp for its new task.

Much like Kylee.

She'd shed her skin more than once before. First with her family moving from royalty to commoners. Next with transforming herself from the Student Most Likely to Succeed into the cliché good girl who ran off with the bad boy. Try as she might, she could never get that role to fit. But neither could she pull on her old skin of Girl at the Head of the Class. Now she had to forge a new identity in this company, and she was determined it wouldn't be the Kid at the Back of the Class who didn't know the material.

Kylee rolled up her sleeves and prepared to get to work. Of course, her cell phone chose that moment to ring. She looked down at the number. It looked vaguely familiar.

"Mrs. Romano?" said the voice on the other end.

"No," Kylee said, shaking her head for further emphasis even though the person on the other end of the receiver couldn't see her. "I mean, yes. I was Kylee Romano. I go by Bauer now."

"Mrs. Bauer-"

"No. I mean, yes. I'm no longer married. It's Ms. Bauer."

There was a pregnant pause. "Ms. Bauer?"

"Yes."

"This is Mrs. Ackerman from Barton Elementary School. I'm calling about your daughter."

Kylee didn't panic. She didn't immediately think the worst. She doubted that her child had fallen into danger and been harmed. Instead, Kylee sighed and caught her forehead in her palm. "What has Molly done now?"

"She was sent to the principal's office this afternoon. He'd like to have a word with you. Can you come in?"

Kylee couldn't leave work just now. She had to turn in this project. But first, she had to understand the software, get her test questions into the software, and figure out where the send button was so that she could submit it to her boss. "I'll be by to pick her up after school."

"He'd like to meet with you before then, if possible."

"I'm sorry, I can't leave work right now."

There was another pregnant pause. But Kylee was used to them. She was determined not to let that silence judge her. Unfortunately, the silence was louder than her resolve. "Fine. I'll be there in an hour."

Molly acting up at yet another school was the last thing Kylee needed. The jokes her daughter liked to play and the mischief she liked to cause were all from her father's side of the family, make no mistake about it. Kylee knew the divorce had been hard on Molly. But so had the years of moving around and not knowing where the next meal was coming from.

They were stable now. There would be no more moving now that she was back in her hometown of Adalia, which was just to the north of Cordoba's capital city. Here, bike paths lined every two-lane street and recreational areas for the young and young at heart were at every corner. Kylee was determined to give Molly the same kind of upbringing that she'd had, right down to the small cottage sized castle fit for a disinherited prince. The two story house even had a couple of turrets atop the roof.

Unlike her own parents, when Molly entered the dating years, Kylee was going to scrutinize every guy that came along. If he wore a motorcycle jacket, was in a band, or any other cliché that bad boys cloaked themselves in to trick good girls, Kylee was going to kick his little booty to the curb so fast.

Molly would be a good girl. And there would be no James Dean wannabes hanging around her daughter. There would not be a repeat mistake of that. In fact, Kylee was certain she would never date again herself.

CHAPTER TWO

The day had been cloudy, but as Ron stepped out of the cafeteria, the clouds broke, and the sun came out. A blue jay perched on the cherry blossom tree outside the doorway to the lunchroom and began a sweet tune. Ron hummed along, pursing his lips in time to the tweets.

Kylee Bauer was back in town.

"Principal Kidd, someone stuffed a Harry Potter book in the toilet in the bathroom in the upper hall. There's water all over the place."

"Cool. That's good," Ron said patting the head janitor on his back.

Not only was Kylee Bauer back in town, but she was minus a wannabe James Dean husband. Ron had never liked Jason Romano and his ultra gelled hair, and his misquoting of Lord Byron love poems, or his motorcycle jacket and motorcycle, and did he mention the gelled, black hair.

Back when they were in high school, Jason would rev his motorcycle engine loud in the school parking lot to make sure everyone knew he had arrived. Ron and Kylee used to roll their eyes at the delinquent as he went out with cheerleaders and popular girls and even a couple of teachers. Kylee had always said she'd never fall for a guy like that.

And then she did.

"We just had two more violin bridges break. The piano needs another tuning, plus some keys are stuck and one pedal isn't working. And I just found a hole in the drum this morning."

Ron nodded in earnest as Ms. Dawsey, the school music and choral instructor droned on and on, trailing him down the hall.

Ron had been crushed the day Kylee had started dating Jason. Ron Kidd and Kylee Bauer had been best friends since elementary school when he'd loaned her a Number 2 pencil and she'd loaned him a pencil top eraser. He'd been in love since that day.

The two had been inseparable during middle school, and high school. Except for the second half of senior year when Jason had set his sights on Kylee.

At the start of Senior year, Ron had finally drummed up the courage to ask Kylee out. But on the very day he'd planned to make his move, he'd found Kylee standing next to Jason who was sitting on his motorcycle. She'd leaned in and kissed him, and Ron's entire world came to a crashing halt.

It was so cliché. Good girl and bad boy. It was something out of one of those American filmmaker John Hughes movie.

Ron hated John Hughes movies. The good girl always got the guy, but it was always the wrong guy. Everyone knew Ducky was the better choice. And the Geek in *Sixteen Candles* would grow up to be a better provider. Same for *The Breakfast Club*.

In fact, wasn't the geek the same actor in both of those films? In any case, all Ron knew was that both the jock and the delinquent were likely working dead-end jobs, but the geek had likely built an empire now.

Kylee had agreed with him in his reviews of John Hughes' films, though she made him watch them all at least twice a year since middle school. At least she'd said she had agreed with him back then. But most girls he knew wanted the jock, the delinquent, the bad boy. No one ever dated the principal.

"Hey, Ronnie."

The sultry voice was out of place in an elementary school filled with energetic adolescent voices and enthused educators. Ron looked up to see Iman Hilson. Iman was another throwback to his high school days. But back then he was beneath the notice of the Head Cheerleader, Prom Queen, Most Popular Girl in School. But after her glory days, Iman divorced the soccer phenom, who didn't turn pro after college. Now she was hot for a teacher.

"Little Ricky is having problems with math," Iman said, siding up to Ron in her low-cut blouse and high slit skirt. "I was wondering if you could come over and tutor him tonight. I remember you used to tutor me in high school."

"We have a number of great tutors in the after-school program," said Ron stepping around her. But he didn't get far. Even though she was wearing six-inch heels.

"I think a little one-on-one would be best for my kid. You always say you want to do what's best for the kids."

"I do say that," Ron agreed as he maneuvered

them towards the main entrance. Most days his focus was on the inner workings of the school, but today he was focused on what was coming into the school. "I will do what's best for Ricky, Jr. I'll arrange that after-school tutor and I'll be sure and check on his progress myself."

Ron knew for a fact that, despite the dysfunction in his home, Ricky, Jr. was an excellent student. The fourth grader was attentive, eager to please, though hopelessly un-athletic.

"I just stopped in to drop off the new pitch packet from Here 2 Learn," said Iman. "I know it's a formality as Barton Elementary has been a loyal customer for the last five years."

"I've told your boss that we are looking at other options," said Ron.

"Can't we talk about this over a glass of wine later tonight?"

"I'm allergic."

Not to the wine. He was allergic to any woman who'd try to use her feminine wiles to seduce him into making a decision, especially one where his job and the children in his care were of concern. And anyone who would think he would even consider it was not someone he would ever want to be associated with.

"Would you excuse me?" Ron ducked out of that trap of Iman and took a step towards the main entrance. Where he promptly halted in his tracks.

It was something out of a John Hughes movie, complete with an anxiety-filled eighties track. The sun acted as a backlight as the doors parted and let her through. She moved in slow motion and Ron's heart stopped beating. Stars twinkled in his eyes. The whole scene went foggy and dream-like from a montage that would later be cut together and remixed just before the final scene of the movie where the two lovers realize they belong together.

Coming into the double doors and back into his life was the only woman Ron had ever loved. Kylee Bauer was back in town.

CHAPTER THREE

Kylee's car came to a sputtering stop as she approached the school zone. She put the car in park and prayed that it would start up again. The last thing she needed was another mechanic bill. Her father might've left her her childhood home, but it came with a repair bill and no other royal inheritance.

Jason had sworn that he'd had the car looked at on its regular maintenance schedule. But like so many things in their relationship, she doubted that was entirely true.

They'd sold Kylee's first car one year into their marriage. It had been Kylee's graduation present from her parents. But Jason said they could ride his bike most of the time or take the bus when it rained. So, she agreed. And then she got pregnant.

This current model car was a far cry from the new model her father had proudly handed her the keys to nearly ten years ago. Kylee stepped out of the car with a squeak of the door hinges. The sun was high in the sky, shining brightly off her old elementary school. Visions of her first day here at Barton flashed in her head.

She'd been so excited to come to school, but also scared. It had seemed huge. Most elementary schools were single or two-story buildings on a few acres of land. Not so in the city of Adalia.

Beyond the elementary school, Kylee spied the middle school and high school. Adalia had a cluster model. The thinking was that it made transitioning for the kids easier. All Kylee remembered was feeling intimidated that first day.

There were other royal children in the halls. Like most modern royals, the highborn easily mixed with the middle class as the commoners often had more status and wealth in this age. Though Kylee's father was a distant relation to the King, there was little to no contact between the families. Kylee's father lived in happy disgrace with his divorcee wife who hadn't been entirely single when they fell in love. But just as Marilee Bauer had done as she walked away from the palace with her prince, Kylee had kept her head high as she'd walked the halls.

Those feelings of intimidation soon passed, and Kylee had excelled as she'd transitioned to each of the buildings on the Barton school campus. She'd been an academic superstar when she'd been enrolled here. Now she felt like a washed up has-been. Her star had pretty much fizzled after graduation. But it was a new day and she was entering the cluster a new woman... with a troubled kid in tow.

Kylee scrubbed her hands over her face as she took the four steps to the double doors. Then she pressed her hands down her skirt hoping to smooth away any wrinkles on the fabric. She'd never been in trouble a day in her life while she was in school. Sure, she'd been in the principal's office many times. But each time had been to receive praise for an accomplishment, accolade, or honor.

This would not be one of those times. Ms. Most Likely to Succeed had failed. And now her kid was a troublemaker.

Kylee pushed her way through the double doors of the school. She was shocked to find that the school smelled the same, it looked the same, it felt the same. There was a chill in the halls that had her wishing for one of her old cardigans. But she'd ditched those prim cover-ups, as well as her tiara, when Jason had draped his leather jacket around her shoulders.

Just inside the double doors was a showcase that had been on display since Kylee's days at Barton. It was each fifth-grade graduating class photo going back for over fifty years. She found her fifth-grade picture among the dozens. She stared for a long moment at the innocence in that little girl's eyes.

Then, in the reflection, she saw a vision of herself sitting alone. But Kylee had never been alone in school. She wasn't popular, but she'd had a group of friends throughout her entire school career. She'd even had a best friend. But she hadn't seen him in years. She'd let that relationship run fallow along with much of her old life in Adalia.

The vision of herself shifted and Kylee realized she was looking at her daughter in the present. Kylee turned to find Molly sitting alone outside the main office. Her heart broke to see her kid sitting so with her arms crossed over her small chest, but her head held high and proud. Just like her royal ancestors.

Kylee had stayed in one place as a kid. She'd

been secure with parents who loved each other and her. She'd had a community she was safe in.

Molly had had none of that. But things would be different now. Kylee would give all of that to her daughter. Normalcy. No more leather jackets and motorcycles. No more half-baked ideas and no follow through. Heck, no more men period.

"Hey, Molls."

"Hey, Mommy."

Kylee slumped down into the empty seat next to her daughter. "So, whatcha been up to?"

A flush crept across her little girl's cheeks. "I made a poor decision. But you don't have to worry. I didn't like the consequences, so I won't do it again."

Kylee opened her mouth and then closed it. She hadn't planned what sage advice she'd give her kid. She didn't even know what had happened to bring Molly to the principal's attention. But it would appear the moral was taught, and the lesson learned. Adalia was already working its magic.

"I talked with the principal," Molly continued. "He's really nice and really funny. I think you'd like him and-"

"Kylee Bauer."

The voice that said her name was deep and resounding. But there was something comfortingly familiar about it. Kylee turned to see a tall, broad man with bright eyes full of patience, a warm smile ready to deliver a punchline, and the silver-gray hair of someone wise beyond his years.

The man was handsome, to be sure. But it was the kindness in his eyes that threatened Kylee's resolve to swear off men for life. He held open his arms and before she knew it, she was swept into a hug.

Kylee forgot to protest. It had been so long since she'd been held. It couldn't hurt if she allowed one more second of the comfort before she told this stranger off.

"It's so good to see you again," he said.

"It is?" Kylee asked.

"I've missed you so much."

"You have?"

The gray-haired man pulled away but didn't release her from his embrace. He rested his hands on her shoulders and grinned down at her. Did she mention that he was tall? And handsome? With the cutest lopsided grin and…

"Oh my gosh, Ron? Ronald Kidd? Is that you?"

"I believe it is, your highness. Unless you let total strangers hug you."

"I do. I mean, I don't." Kylee took a deep breath

to ward off all the fluster. It didn't help. "It's so good to see you again. It's been so long. I've missed you so much."

Kylee shut her mouth when she realized she was parroting everything Ron had already said. Instead, she went back into his arms. This time she gave him a proper hug, one that was fit to greet her old best friend.

But, oh wow, had her best friend filled out. Ron had been a lanky teen, all limbs and sinew. Kylee felt muscles when her cheek met his chest. Same on his back where her fingers gave him a squeeze. That warm and spicy scent on him hadn't been there when he was an adolescent or a teen.

Now Kylee's cheeks warmed. She was sure they were a bright shade of pink and she ducked her head when she pulled away out of Ron's embrace. "It's really good to see you, Old Man."

"You too, Ace."

"Ace?" asked Molly.

Kylee had nearly forgotten about her daughter sitting there. That was rare. Molly wasn't the quiet type of kid, but she was sitting silently, watching the exchange between old friends.

"Your mom, here, has never failed a test. She

always got an A. So, I called her Ace when we were kids."

"I get it," said Molly. "And she called you Old Man because of the gray hair."

Canities ran in the Kidd family. One of God's great ironies to put a premature graying gene in a family of humans who go by a youthful last name. The old Lord Kidd had been the jolliest of Santas ever since he was in his twenties.

"Imagine my surprise when I found myself having a heart-to-heart with your mini-me," Ron said.

Kylee looked from Ron to her daughter. Molly had a mischievous glint in her eye, one that reminded Kylee of her dad. It was a glint that said *I'm about to be up to no good*.

"I'm so sorry for whatever trouble she's caused," said Kylee. "It's been hard on her with the move and… everything."

Did Ron know she was divorced? She was sure he did. It was a small town. And she was still a royal, regardless of how far removed she was. Her divorce had been mentioned in a gossip rag. It had only been a couple of sentences, but it had still been there in black and white.

Kylee was sure all the residents had been kept

abreast of every misstep and failing in her marriage. It was one reason why Kylee had never come back home after her decision to run off with the town bad boy with no name, connection, or coins to rub together. She'd been every cliche of a good girl falls for the rebel. Except her life had continued after the last page, after the credits rolled. No one had said anything about bills, and arguments, and infidelities in those Hallmark dramas.

Ron had been one of the most vocal people to tell her not to go. He'd insisted she'd be sorry. Kylee had been stubborn, certain she could make it work, certain she could reform the bad boy and make him into a family man. It was the one and only time in her life that she'd gotten the answer to a problem wrong.

"Are you kidding?" Ron was saying. "Molly here is one of the smartest kids I've ever meant. I think she's gonna give you a run for your money in the academic department, Ace. Just know, Ms. Molly, that your mom's are big shoes to fill."

Kylee's breath caught. It had been so long since she'd received praise. Ron had always been there with a supportive word, or the notes when she'd missed class, or ready to work through a difficult problem with her. And he always did it with a smile on his face and a joke on his lips.

Ron was frowning at Kylee now. His gaze focused down on the floor. "Though I'm not sure about those shoes you've got on there. Those look pretty big."

Kylee reached over and gave him a shove in the shoulder. Ron chuckled as she did so. His laughter was so infectious that Kylee caught herself laughing too. It was the first time she'd laughed in…she couldn't remember how long.

Looking over she saw her daughter laughing as well. Kylee couldn't remember the last time Molly had laughed either.

The twinkle in Molly's eyes was even brighter. Maybe it wasn't mischief her daughter was up to. Maybe she was just happy? At this moment, basking in Ron's light praise and silly humor, Kylee certainly felt happy herself.

CHAPTER FOUR

How could a person grow more beautiful?

Ron had heard Kylee called an understated beauty by adults when they were younger. He'd never understood the need for the qualifier. He'd always seen her as beautiful, from the first day they met in kindergarten.

Back then he'd shared his Cheetos snack pack with her. Every kid knew that a Cheetos snack pack was a prized snack in the school lunch box. Ron only shared with Kylee.

He'd been an awkward kid, unable to relate to anyone his own age. He'd always been great with kids though. It was inevitable that he ended up in his current position.

The only person his age that had understood him had been Kylee. Whereas Ron got kids and loved learning, Kylee got tests and loved learning. He'd always known they'd been made for each other. And now he had the chance to present his assessment to her.

"You look amazing, Kylee," Ron said.

A deep blush colored Kylee's cheek. He could always make her blush, but mostly from laughing. He needed to show her he was no longer her silly pal. He was a grown man who was willing and able to be a true partner to her.

"You've grown up so much, too," she said. "Still wearing suits, I see."

"The suit makes the man."

Ron had always dressed for the part he wanted to play in life. That was the part of principal. And he'd finally achieved that lifelong dream. Now his other dream was standing before him. All he could think of doing was reaching out and grabbing her.

He swept his hand out in front of his torso, as though he were making a presentation. "Would you like to step into my office so we can talk?"

Kylee's huge grin wobbled a bit. She turned back to her daughter, giving Molly what Ron knew was the *what-have-you-done-to-embarrass-the- family-*

look. Ron would set Kylee straight on Molly's behavior. He knew the kid was just acting out to find her place. Ron had every intention of convincing both Molly and Kylee that they'd found exactly where they belonged.

They walked past the phone receptionist, and the attendance receptionist, and his principal's assistant. Each woman failed miserably at hiding their interest. Or so Ron thought. No one knew about his crush on Kylee. Well, except for his parents.

Once they got behind closed doors, Ron watched Kylee as she looked around his office. It both thrilled and scared him to view his office through her eyes. He wondered what she thought of his many accomplishments since they'd last talked. He knew what she had been doing. He'd kept in regular contact with her parents up until their deaths a year ago. The town had mourned their passing, even though they had moved to the south of the country.

"Wow, I didn't know you earned your PhD." Kylee said fingering the frame of his degree.

"My EdD, too. But it's out being framed."

She turned and her eyes went wide. "Two doctorates? Overachiever."

Ron was usually bashful in the light of others'

praise. But his chest swelled with pride under Kylee's perusal. He'd always rushed to show her the Good Job sticker he'd earned, or the string of A-pluses on his report card, or the handwritten notes on a particularly good essay.

"Dr. Kidd? Wow. I always knew you'd achieve your dreams."

Ron motioned her into a seat. But instead of sitting in his chair, he sat beside her, in the same seat her daughter had occupied only an hour ago. Their knees bumped and Ron felt a crackle of electricity.

"And you?" he said. "Has the College Board swept you up yet? One of the elite to get perfect scores on their tests each time she took it. They must want you in-house to figure out how you did it."

"No," she looked down. "Not the College Board. I'm working at a small test prep company. They're called Thrive to Learn Systems. They have a lot of innovative ideas."

"Kylee that's amazing. So, you'll be in town for a while."

She nodded. "We're here to stay. Molly and me. Not…"

Well, that answered that question. Her ex was well and truly out of the picture. The road was clear for Ron.

"Ron, about Molly?"

"Hmm? Oh, right, Molly. She's a great kid."

"But she was called to the principal's office. Her teacher sent me an email about something to do with a ruler a couple of days ago?"

"It's nothing to worry about. Molly's just trying to figure out her place here. I think she'll be fine."

"Really?"

"Have I ever steered you wrong?"

"No. No, you haven't."

Kylee chewed at her lower lip. Ron's gaze fixed to the motion. He'd dreamed of kissing her since he'd seen it done on television.

He hadn't dated a lot of women in the last decade. Mainly because no one ever measured up to the dream of simply kissing Kylee. And here she was in the flesh, tugging at the oh so bitable center of her bottom lip.

Kylee let go of her lip. Their gazes met. Ron watched as her breath caught. She'd caught him staring. He'd give anything to know what she was thinking right now. She wasn't frowning. Maybe the thought of him thinking about kissing her wasn't unappetizing.

This was the perfect moment to find out. Not to kiss her. But to ask her out so that it might lead to that first kiss. Ron opened his mouth… and a knock sounded at the door.

His secretary poked her head in. "The bell is about to ring, and they need you for bus duty since Mr. Martin is still on paternity leave with his wife."

Ron swallowed down his desire. It was hard to pass. "I'll be right there."

Kylee stood. "I'm sorry. I've been keeping you from your duties."

Ron stood too. "Not at all. I always have time for you."

They were standing close enough for him to smell the berry scent of her shampoo. She tugged at her lower lip again. This time the right corner.

She gazed up at him. It was clear her tongue was tied. "It's really good to see you again, Old Man."

"You said that already, Ace."

"Well, it's true. I really missed you."

"Said that too."

She smiled and then she moved to the door. Then she took a half step toward him. It looked as though she were about to give him another hug. But in the light of the open door, she retreated and stepped around him. "I'll see you around, okay?"

Before she could cross the threshold, Ron blurted out, "Kylee, we should see each other again."

She paused and turned. So did the phone receptionist, and the attendance receptionist, and the principal's assistant.

"To catch up," Ron clarified for the prying ears. "It's been ten years. We've spent less than ten minutes together. How about dinner?"

"Dinner?"

"Buster and Eden's is still open."

"Are you serious? I can't believe the health inspectors haven't closed that place down."

"What are you talking about? Best chili dogs in all of Cordoba."

"I..."

"Principal Kidd?" said his assistant. "They need you."

Ron looked from his assistant, then around the main office quickly filling with teachers, kids, and parents, and back to Kylee. He couldn't press his pursuit of her in front of all these people. "We'll talk soon, okay."

"Sure."

And with that, she collected her daughter and

headed to the main door. Molly looked over her shoulder and offered Ron a wink.

He'd seen Jason give that wink to many a girl. He'd seen it work to make Kylee stray. But on the kid, it was adorable, and it only made him like her more.

CHAPTER FIVE

The smell of burned broccoli filled the kitchen. Kylee pulled the back door open to let the smell out. But the wind didn't dare venture inside the kitchen.

Kylee had never been the best cook. Jason had reminded her of that time and again. But now that she was back in her childhood home where her mom had placed so many delectable dinners on the table, she wanted to try and emulate that for her daughter.

"Mommy, can't we just go to McDonald's?"

Another fault of Jason's. Here they lived in one of the most culturally diverse nations in the entire world where walking down any street the spicy smells of Indian dhals, the toasty smell of rising French croissants, and the bitter aroma of Ethiopian coffee beans would seduce the nose. Yet her ex had been a fan of American fast foods that had bullied their way onto the Main Streets.

"No, we're having a home-cooked meal," said Kylee.

Molly moaned and whined and pretty soon the smoke alarm joined her. Kylee tugged off her checkered apron which read "Hot Stuff Coming Through." She turned off the burners and yanked open the refrigerator.

Five minutes later, dinner was served. She'd slapped together some peanut butter and jelly sandwiches along with some orange slices and a glass of milk. All food groups were covered.

"Great cooking, chef," said Molly around a mouthful of choke sandwich.

"Oh, hush you Molly-monster."

Molly giggled. Kylee found herself laughing as she swiped a dollop of strawberry jam off her thumb. It might not be gourmet, but it sure was fine dining. This was just what they needed.

Dinners had been a tense affair the last few months of her marriage. Money had always been tight. Anything could set Jason off and launch into an argument that would end with a door being slammed and him being gone for the night, and sometimes into the next day.

But there was no slamming of doors tonight. The fire alarm was quiet now that Kylee had backed away from the kitchen appliances. It was a peaceful, nutritiously-questionable, night at the Bauer castle. But Kylee still had to parent.

"So, Molly, what exactly got you sent to the principal's office today?"

"Fairy magic," Molly said as she pressed the rind of an orange into her mouth and gave her mother a citrus smile.

Her daughter had the wildest imagination. Kylee envied her that. Kylee had always been a black and white kind of girl. That's why she did so well with tests and numbers. Meanwhile, Molly spent time making curly cues with the L's and Y in her name.

"Molls, you have to take learning seriously. It's how you'll have a good future."

"I'm only in fourth grade, Mommy. Don't I have years before my future starts?"

Sometimes, Kylee worried her daughter was too much like her father. Head-in-the-clouds dreamer with no practical know how. At least Molly had a can-do kinda attitude. Even if her doing typically got her into trouble. Now that Jason was less of an influence in her life, Kylee would change that.

"Besides, Principal Kidd set me straight," Molly said after taking a gulp of her milk. "We've got it all worked out."

"Do you now?"

It was so strange hearing her old best friend being referred to in such a lofty status. But Ron had always been great with kids. He didn't really have a choice with the last name he had.

"Yeah, he's really funny, don't ya think?"

Kylee smiled. Ron always had a way of making her take herself less seriously. The two had been an inseparable pair for more than half her life. Seeing him again, that old connection felt ready to slip right back into place. In a way, it felt like they'd never been apart at all.

"We should have him over for dinner one night."

It would be nice to have Ron back in her life on a regular basis. To sit next to him, and talk to him, and get another one of those hugs.

Ron's embrace had been so warm, so inviting. It had felt so good to be held, and by someone, whom she knew had only her best interests in heart. In fact, her heart was racing at the memory of being in his arms.

Wait? In his arms? That made it almost sound intimate.

It wasn't intimate. He was Ron. Her buddy. Her friend.

Her buddy who had grown into a fine young man - emphasis on fine. Her friend whose gaze had slipped down to look at her lips. He'd looked at her and talked to her like she was the only person in the world. And when he'd asked her to dinner, her heart had actually skipped a beat.

It was madness. It was insane. He was Ron. Her heart should not be skipping a beat at Ron.

But it had.

But she couldn't date Ron.

He was the principal at her daughter's school. And he was her best friend. And it was too soon after her divorce. And he was a man. And she'd sworn off men for the rest of her life.

Plus, she was certain Ron wasn't interested in her that way. He'd just been paying attention to her like he always did. He'd looked at her lips before. He'd hugged her before. It meant nothing.

Ron was a great success. Meanwhile, Kylee had been brought low just as everyone had warned her would happen if she continued on with Jason. Ron had achieved all of his dreams. Meanwhile, Kylee was just getting started, ten years late.

But it would be nice to have him as a friend again.

"You thinking about Principal Kidd?"

Kylee glanced over to see her daughter smiling with that mischievous glint in her eyes.

"His eyes totally lit up when he found out you were my mom. Just like Scooby Doo when he sees a Scooby Snack."

Really? Just like Scooby Doo?

"Now your eyes are going all Scoobied."

Kylee gave herself a shake and began clearing away dishes. "Ron -Principal Kidd and I... we're just friends."

"Best friends?"

"We used to be." Kylee turned on the faucet to wash away the excess jelly from a plate.

"Maybe now that you're older, you could be more?"

Oh. Oh no. Oh no, no, no.

Was that what the mischievous look was all about? Was Molly trying to play matchmaker between her mom and the principal? Kylee had to nip that in the bud.

But by the time she'd turned around Molly was gone. She'd have a talking-to with her daughter soon enough. Because dating, much less marriage, was the last thing that was on Kylee's mind.

CHAPTER SIX

Ron hated faculty meetings. He'd hated them when he was a teacher. He hated them even more as an administrator. Even now, when he was in charge of running the meeting, he wanted to be anywhere but in the school conference room.

He was constantly buried in paperwork, on the phone with concerned parents, getting an earful from teachers and their needs, facing issues with the school building itself, and then there were the kids. He'd rather be actively participating in any of those other activities than being trapped in an endless meeting.

Thankfully, the meeting was coming to a close. The teachers were all itching to get on the road before the rush hour hit. But when Mrs. Steen rose, a collective sigh rang around the room.

"We need to begin preparing for the state standardized tests," said Mrs. Steen.

Jaws tensed, strained temples were rubbed, and tired eyes were rolled. For once Ron wasn't the bad guy in the room. There was a perception that when a teacher left the classroom to join the Main Office they were going to the dark side. As if now he was on the wrong side of The Force. But they were all on the same side with the same goals; to be a force for good for the children of their community.

Aside from the common ground of wanting their students to succeed, most teachers had little appreciation for standardized testing. The current state and national testing systems were more of a comparison made amongst schools than an assessment of student achievement and areas for improvement. So, in essence, the teachers were being tested.

"We all know the Board of Education wants data-driven results when it comes to testing," Mrs. Steen continued.

"But that shouldn't mean they can control what we do in our classroom," said Mr. Collins, another veteran of the school system that had been around when Ron was a student in these halls himself. "We take up so much time preparing for these standardized tests we don't have any time to actually teach."

Ron agreed. In the span of two decades, education had changed so drastically. He'd taken a couple of standardized tests in his formative years. But they'd all been to collect data to help teachers teach better. None of them had determined how much funding his school would receive or give Barton a grade that prospective parents would weigh in deciding where they wanted their future students to attend. Certainly, none had determined the job security of his teachers or the entire school.

Nowadays principals were caught between the Board of Education who wanted data-driven results, the teachers who wanted control of their classrooms, and parents who wanted to see their kids succeed. But it was the new policy, and Ron had to push the policy.

"We need to have everyone handing in lesson plans every week to make sure all the children are getting an adequate education," said Mrs. Steen.

"The requirement is not for weekly lesson plans," Ron spoke up. "You can turn them in unit by unit."

"But we need to be sure to evaluate," said Mrs. Steen.

"There is no requirement to evaluate everyone's lesson and make them similar," said Ron. "Where you have a strength, Mr. Collins might have a weakness."

"Weaknesses shouldn't be tolerated when it comes to the future of our community," she said.

"Forgive me," said Ron. "Weakness is the wrong word. We all have our own strengths. If we use those strengths to teach the lesson, the children will get what they need."

There was a rally of head nods and grunts of agreement. Ron had worked hard to earn the trust of the people gathered around. He'd worked with most of them for the last decade either being one of their students, helping in their classes as a teaching assistant during college, or being a colleague.

He may have been young, but he'd proven himself in the halls, conferences, and of course the endless meetings. They knew he understood where they were coming from and would have their interest at heart.

"We still have to evaluate the new test prep company," said Mrs. Steen.

"We already have a prep company," said Mr.

Collins. "We've been with Here 2 Learn for the last five years."

"And for the last two years, we've had problems with the company providing us outdated material, lessons that didn't meet the competencies, and late delivery of results."

Half of the room nodded in agreement at Mrs. Steen's assessment of the test prep company. The other half crossed their arms and fidgeted with the pens and papers in their hands, clearly uncomfortable with change.

"There's a new company that's getting some attention," Mrs. Steen continued. "They're called Thrive Learning Systems and they've been using very innovative testing methods."

Ron perked up when he heard the name of the company. He remembered it because it had been uttered by Kylee's lips. He'd paid very good attention to her mouth when she'd been speaking. When she'd been quiet, too.

"We don't need to try anything new now," said Mr. Collins. "Let's stick with the known."

"No, actually," said Ron, sitting up taller and commanding the room once more, "I think we should look into this new company. Besides if Here 2

Learn knows it's got competition, that might encourage them to make improvements."

There were more nods of assent than shrugs, so Ron took it as a good sign.

"If that's all," he said, "we can adjourn the meeting."

Every teacher gathered his or her stack of papers and rose. Except for Mrs. Steen. Ever since he'd been chosen as the newest principal of Barton two years ago, she'd been on his back. Suddenly, the thought of Molly Romano putting glitter on her eraser brightened Ron's mood.

"I want to put a few things on the agenda for the next staff meeting," she said. "We're still facing overcrowding in the classes."

"There's been population growth in the city," he said. "I'm looking to hire more teachers, but there are budget constraints."

"You've spent a lot of that budget on anti-bullying when some of us believe it should go to test prep."

"We have the budget meeting coming up at the end of the school year and I will be happy to take your concerns then, Mrs. Steen."

"There's also the issue of the Romano girl. If I'm going to prepare my students for this test, I can't have antics like that in my class. She might fare better in Mr. Collin's class."

"I'm not moving her from your class." As much as he wanted to. Molly might challenge her authority, but Ron knew Mrs. Steen was one of the best teachers on his roster. A bright kid like Molly needed the challenge that only she could bring. Still, he felt sorry for the kid. "The two of you need to find a way to get along."

Mrs. Steen didn't look happy. Her jaw tensed and he saw her grinding her molars. Ron remembered her doing that in his youth when she was thinking up the perfect punishment for a naughty student.

"If I remember correctly, you and the Romano girl's mother were quite close in your youth."

"Kylee. Kylee Bauer. We were friends through our entire school years."

"Princess Kylee," Mrs. Steen sneered.

Ron had heard that Mrs. Steen's distant ancestors had held a dukedom. But none of the wealth or status had trickled down the bloodline to her.

Ron had never thought much about Kylee being royal. She'd been noble in her actions. That's what had always counted for him.

"She's divorced now, I understand?"

Ron didn't nod. He wasn't sure where this was going, but he felt that he was back in Mrs. Steen's class and she was setting him up.

"Of course, you know it's against school policy to date any of the parents."

Ron only raised an eyebrow, but it was clear Mrs. Steen knew she'd gotten under his skin. He did know that policy. He'd used that line a few times on some of the single moms of the PTA, and once with an unhappily married one. But he hadn't considered it when Kylee had stepped into his office and back into his life. He wasn't sure he wanted to consider the ramifications now.

CHAPTER SEVEN

Kylee was great at tests. She got a perfect score on the SATs four times. She'd never needed to truly study. Once she was told information, she cataloged it in her head, and it stayed in its compartment. When she needed it, she was able to open that cabinet and pull out the details again.

She didn't have a photographic memory. The visuals of her past were often hazy. But she could remember large swaths of information for long periods of time. And she had excellent organizational skills.

That, along with a true passion for knowledge, enabled her to ace every test she met. Tests were just a system. A system that had made sense to her since her first spelling bee.

She got a thrill when she looked down at the bubbles of a multiple-choice test. She was excited to fill in a blank. The sound of a timer ticking away on a teacher's desk had never made her sweat. It had always presented a challenge.

Kylee was well-versed in all forms of testing. But these new standardized tests to measure the effectiveness of the education system was a tricky beast. These tests didn't so much measure the individual kid's skill as it measured the effectiveness of the test and the teachers of the tests. The standards didn't measure the uniqueness of the test taker so much as they measured the similarity of them.

Crafting lessons and assessments to prepare kids for these standardized tests was a true challenge. A challenge she'd been shaky on her first few days at Thrive Learning Systems. But now that she'd cracked the code to get into the computer system, it was a challenge she was up for. And like all problems presented to her, Kylee was prepared to ace this one.

"Ms. Romano?"

"Bauer." Kylee looked up to see the president of the company standing over her desk.

Syd Rowen was in his late forties. But his hair was already graying. Still, there was something about him that cast a youthful air. Or perhaps it was all the twenty-somethings he employed in his company. Mr. Rowen and Kylee were easily the two oldest people in the entire building.

In the two weeks she'd been here, she'd only met him once. That was on her first day. He'd been behind closed doors ever since.

There could only be one reason he was coming to her now. She'd messed up somehow, and he was going to fire her. Great. What would she do now?

Kylee only had a small amount of money left to her by her parents. And the house. Which needed repairs. She could go to her extended family and throw herself at their mercy. Things had changed in the upper echelons of the royal kingdom since her father had been shunned.

Kylee pressed her palms to her office chair preparing to rise and head into Mr. Rowen's office for a private word that could be a reprimand or a termination. But instead of waving her to his office, Mr. Rowen pulled up a spare chair and sat down beside her.

"I was looking through your file and saw that you're from the city of Adalia."

"Yes. I was born and raised here."

"Do you know much about Clara Barton Elementary School?"

"I... uh... Yes. I went there as a child."

Mr. Rowen frowned, scratching at the hair on his chin. "So, a few decades ago. You won't likely have kept in touch with anyone there."

A few decades? She hadn't even been alive for a few decades. He was wrong about her age, but he was right about her not keeping in touch. "I just moved back there. My daughter is enrolled at Barton Elementary."

Mr. Rowen's frown lifted a bit. Kylee supposed that was his rendition of a smile. "You might be able to help me out with something."

"Of course," Kylee offered. Since they were sitting out in the public area of cubicles, she assumed she was safe from a pink slip. She was game for anything that could guarantee her continued employment.

Mr. Rowen leaned forward, placing his elbows on his knees. "We are looking to win a contract with the school system in Adalia. Do you know any of the administrators there at the elementary school? Perhaps your child's teacher?"

"I... uh..." Kylee didn't want to have any more chats with Mrs. Steen. She felt bad she had to send Molly to that class every day. Luckily, she also knew an administrator. If there was anyone Kylee wanted to reach out to and see again, it was Ron. "Um, I know the principal at Barton. He and I went to school together."

Mr. Rowen's brows raised to his hairline. The movement of those facial muscles in the upper part of his face lifted the ones in the lower part of his face. He looked like he was kinda, sorta smiling. "Do you think you could set up a meeting with the principal?"

"Um, sure. I just met with him yesterday."

"That's excellent."

"We hadn't seen each other in a long time, so we'd said we'd make plans to go out to dinner. He suggested we go to an old restaurant that we used to go to as kids called-"

"That's excellent, Ms. Bauer. Follow up with him. See if you can work your angles."

Her angles?

"If we can get the elementary school on board

with our company to offer the test prep for the standardized exam that gives us a leg up to contract with the entire county."

Kylee looked to the screen where she was just starting to make headway with the test prep and back to her boss. He wanted her to use her angles to get her old best friend to agree to use Thrive as their test prep company. Was that ethical?

"Can I count on you to take care of this, Ms. Bauer?"

"I... uh..."

Mr. Rowen's mouth thinned into a definite frown. "This would be a big account for this company. If you were the one to get the account, there would definitely be a promotion in your future."

"A promotion?"

"Crafting your own curriculum and assessments with the college prep side of the company instead of the elementary and secondary levels. You could begin working on our SAT and ACT prep courses."

Kylee had never liked back-scratching. As the daughter of an outcast prince who married for love, and now a divorcee from an uncommon jerk, she'd always gotten by on what she knew, not who she knew. But Ron did say he wanted to see her. And help her. They were friends. He would certainly hear her out.

"Can you handle this, Ms. Bauer?"

"Yes, sir. Consider it handled."

CHAPTER EIGHT

"So, you go over the loop, and then pull under." Ron gave Ricky, Jr.'s tie a tug.

"You're choking me, Principal Kidd."

Ron wasn't choking the kid. Like his mother, the little boy did have a flair for the dramatic. Luckily, Ricky, Jr. was one of the lead actors in the school play today.

Ron gave the knot of the tie a tug to loosen it a bit. The kid took a deep inhale and relaxed his small shoulders. "My mom went out last night with a man in a tie. But it looked like a girl's hair ribbons."

"A bow tie?" asked Ron.

Ricky shrugged. "She was dating a musician last week. He never wore ties. His pants had holes and he didn't wear a belt, so his pants hung low enough to see his underwear. Then there was the grandpa she dated."

"Your mom dated a grandpa?" said a light feminine voice.

Molly Bauer turned to face them in her place next to the curtains. She'd come to Barton a couple of weeks after the school year had started, so she didn't have a speaking role. But Barton was inclusive, so she couldn't sit the play out. She was dressed in green to be part of the scenery.

"Ew, your mom dates your grandpa."

"He wasn't my grandpa," insisted Ricky. But even with his suit and tie on for his lead role performance, Ricky couldn't pull off an ounce of menace. "He just had a beard and gray hair like a grandpa. I didn't like him. His skin was wrinkly and he smelled like peppermints. I don't like peppermints. They make my nose itch."

Ron wished it was his place to tell Iman to keep her dating life private from her kid until she was ready to make a commitment to a partner. But his place was not in the home, it was at the school. He could only teach the kids.

"Parents deserve to go out and have fun without their kids," Ron said, deciding to take the diplomatic approach.

"I heard him tell her he wanted to be more than friends," said Ricky. "Whatever that means?"

Ron wanted to shake his head. But he didn't. He opened his mouth to offer more diplomacy, but Molly beat him to the punch.

"What it means is say hello to your new daddy," said Molly.

"But I don't want him to be my daddy," said Ricky. "Or the musician. Or the mechanic. Or the chef."

Now Ron had to put his professional feelings aside and do what was best for the emotional well-being of the child. And a string of men in his life wasn't.

"I want *you* to be my daddy," said Ricky, Jr.

Ron had been down on the kid's level. That statement rocked him back on his heels.

"He can't marry your mom," said Molly. "He's going to marry mine."

That rocked Ron in a totally different way. He barely tolerated Iman. But he couldn't wait to see Kylee again.

"He doesn't even know your mom," said Ricky.

"Yes, he does," said Molly. "They've been best friends their whole lives."

"Is that true, Principal Kidd? Are you gonna marry Molly's mom?"

"I… well…" Ron began. But his mouth wouldn't complete the sentence he knew he was supposed to say. He couldn't deny that he would never marry Kylee. His heart wouldn't let him deny its greatest wish. "Ms. Bauer and I are just friends."

"Teachers can't date parents, dear." All three of them looked up to see Mrs. Steen looming over them. "It's against the rules."

"Says who?" asked Molly.

"Says the boss of the teachers," said Mrs. Steen.

Molly turned to Ron. "I thought you were the boss of the teachers."

"It looks like they need you all on stage," Ron said, taking the cowardly way out. "Have a great show everybody."

Avoiding Mrs. Steen's gaze, Ron rose and made a quick exit from backstage. He took the long route to avoid the other teachers, kids, and parents. He didn't look up or make eye contact with anyone until he reached the back of the auditorium. Once there he leaned against the exit doors. He had an excellent view of the stage and the backs of everyone's heads.

"Why do you look like you're hiding?"

Ron turned to face Kylee. His urge to leave out

the exit doors vanished, and his feet grew roots. "Because I am."

"From who?" she stage-whispered, looking around as though she could find his nemesis.

"Students, teachers, moms."

"Moms?" She turned back to him.

"You may not know this, but I've become a hot commodity these last few years." Ron flipped up the collar of his dress shirt and posed like a model he'd seen in GQ Magazine. "Single professional who's good with kids and has all his hair."

"You sure about that?" Kylee reached up to ruffle his hair.

Ron swatted at her hand. "Hey."

Instead of shoving her hand away, he caught it in his. Somehow, her fingers slid through the gaps his made. To the casual observer, it would clearly look as though they were holding hands.

He'd sat next to Kylee many times in his life and brushed her leg or her shoulder. He'd handed her out of cars a few times. They'd even danced at school functions. They high fived after every test in high school. So, why did he feel like fireworks were going off inside him?

With great reluctance, he pulled his fingers free of hers. "What are you doing here?"

Kylee chucked her thumb towards the front of the auditorium. "My kid's on the stage."

"Right. Of course."

He should mingle with others. Check to see if he was needed anywhere. Chat with a few of the parents. But he stayed put at the back of the room.

"Ron?"

"Hmm?"

"I was actually hoping I could talk to you about something. It's work-related."

"Oh, Molly's doing great today after our talk."

"No, not your work. Mine. I told you the other day that I work for Thrive Learning Systems. We're a test prep company and we're doing very innovative work on test prep for standardized testing. I was hoping to schedule a meeting to pitch you."

"Done."

"Really?" She tipped her head to the side, eyes wide with surprise.

"Really."

"Just like that?" She tipped her head to the other side, grinning hugely with what Ron knew to be giddiness.

"Just like that," he confirmed.

"Because I prepared a whole speech."

Ron chuckled. Of course, Kylee had prepared

and practiced. He took a dramatic inhale and then waved his hand. "Come on, let's have it. Do you want to deliver the speech now?"

"No." She held up her hands in a stop motion. "No need. I already aced it."

"Why don't we talk over dinner tonight?" he said.

"So, I can butter you up?"

"Well, I do like butter."

A parent in the back row turned around and shushed them with a glare. Ron noted a few teachers were watching them from the sidelines. A number of moms in the front row gave Kylee a death glare, which apparently Kylee took notice of.

"Wow," she said. "You weren't kidding about the hot commodity bit. I think I'm gonna go over and sit with the grandmas to, you know, get out of the line of fire."

"See you tonight?" Ron called out to her as she approached an empty seat in the last row.

But when she went to sit down, the mom sitting there suddenly put her purse in the seat. Kylee looked back up at Ron and glared at him, as though it were his fault she no longer had a seat.

It was good-natured joking. And it was. Just joking. Just dinner. Nothing against the rules there.

CHAPTER NINE

"Is that what you're wearing?"

Kylee had begun her descent down the stairs to check on dinner. Molly was in the middle of the staircase, likely headed to her room. The two girls met in the middle.

Molly looked up at her mother. Her round face was contorted in what could only be described as aghast. Kylee looked down at herself in search of what her daughter had found so offensive.

After coming home from a long day of lesson building and problem creating, Kylee had done what she always did. She'd kicked off her heels, slipped out of her confining dress skirt, unbuttoned her starched blouse, discarded her binding bra, and slipped into a pair of yoga pants and a graphic t-shirt.

"He'll be here any minute," said Molly. "You should change. And shower. And for goodness sake put on some makeup. Ricky Wright, Jr.'s mom always has a ton on first thing in the morning when she drops him off."

"What?"

Kylee's head was spinning. Just what was her daughter talking about? Ricky Wright? The only Ricky Wright Kylee knew was the old high school quarterback. She'd heard the rising star had flamed out in college. But she'd also heard that Ricky and Iman Hilson, Adalia's real live mean girl, had had a kid. A boy, if Kylee remembered right. But what did Ricky and Iman's kid have to do with Kylee needing a shower and some makeup?

Kylee leaned against the banister and crossed her arms over her chest. "Molly, what's going on?"

Molly rubbed at a non-existent mark on the wall. "I just think you should look your best tonight when Principal Kidd comes over. You always make me get cleaned and presentable before I go to school every morning. Well, school is coming to our house so you should…" Molly wrinkled her nose and waved her hand at her mom in a shooing motion. "You should really go clean yourself up a bit."

Kylee smoothed a hand over her t-shirt. She had washed her face, reapplied deodorant, and put her bra back on. She was perfectly presentable to have a relaxing evening of catching up with her old friend. "It's just Ron, Principal Kidd. He doesn't care what I'm wearing. He's been here many times before. He practically lived here before you were born."

"Great. Then he'll feel right at home."

There was that sparkle in her daughter's eye again. Jason had had that same sparkle early in their relationship when he'd been sweeping her off her feet. He barely looked at her the last few years of their marriage. And when he did, his eyes were dull with wariness.

Kylee had never walked around as though she had a crown on her head. But after a few years with Jason she'd felt the crown of her head sinking down, and further down into her chest as though her head weighed a ton. It was only in these last few months since the divorce that Kylee had felt a lessening on her shoulders. Her head was nearly back centered between her shoulder blades.

Molly's sparkle told Kylee the little girl was up to something. But what? Kylee had caught her daughter straightening up the living room earlier. It was like pulling teeth to get Molly to do chores. For some reason Molly had done a chore she hadn't been asked to do?

Yes, there was definitely something going on. Maybe she'd gotten into trouble again and suspected Ron would give Kylee the full report tonight? Yes, that had to be it. Before Kylee could start her interrogation, the smoke alarm beat her to it.

Kylee took a deep inhale. The acrid smell of burning food charged into her nostrils. The alarm screamed again demanding attention. Another sound joined the chorus. It was the doorbell.

Kylee looked to Molly. Molly's aghast look was even more pronounced on her round face. In her daughter's eyes, Kylee saw her own mortification.

In unison, they looked at the front door. Then towards the kitchen. Then back to each other.

"You get the door," said Kylee. "I'll get the food."

Kylee dashed off to the kitchen. When she entered, it was too late. The lives of the vegetables were already lost. The pan too, as the greens were now black and putrified in their so-called stainless steel coffin.

"I just remembered," said a deep, male voice

from behind her, "Home Economics is the only class you ever failed."

"I didn't fail," Kylee insisted. "I got a B."

"Only because I was your partner and my A carried you through."

Ron stepped in front of Kylee. He shoved his hand into a pink oven mitt and grabbed the handle of the pan. Moving quickly, he doused the fiery fare in the sink by turning the faucet on full blast.

With the pan contained, Ron returned to the scene of the crime to look for other victims. He turned the oven off where the chicken tenders weren't doing too bad. Frozen dinners that just needed reheating, Kylee could handle. But anything fresh from the ground or the slaughterhouse typically ended up wishing it had been buried six feet under than in her kitchen.

Ron turned to her with a raised eyebrow, a look of admonishment on his face. Kylee couldn't feel chagrined. She was too busy trying to manage the onset of lightheadedness. Not from the smell of smoke. It was from the smell of him.

The spicy smell of Ron cut through the burnt smell of the drenched veggies. Had his jawline always been that sharp? She wondered what the flesh under his chin tasted like? Ron glanced down at her lips as though he were ready to let her nibble.

Kylee jerked her gaze away. What was wrong with her? Ron was her friend. He'd once been her best friend. And she'd just sized him up like he was dinner.

"I'm so sorry dinner's ruined," she said.

"Of course, it's not. I was a Boy Scout, remember."

Kylee glanced behind him at the sink of burnt food. She had no hope anything could be saved. Nothing good to eat was coming out of that fire.

"I came prepared." Ron pointed to the takeout cartons sitting on the breakfast table. He must have deposited them there just before he came to her rescue.

"Really?"

"Really," he snorted. "Don't forget, I know you."

Why did that statement make Kylee feel all warm and tingly inside? But not just warm, also cozy, like she wanted to curl up with Ron on the couch and watch old episodes of *Saved by the Bell* like when they were kids. But this time with a glass of champagne paired with takeout.

She shook herself. That was not what tonight was about. They would be catching up, and then she'd planned to work in a pitch for Thrive. There would be no cozying and no more tingling. Luckily, there would be a buffer between Ron, Kylee, and Kylee's confusing feelings towards her old bestie.

"Molly," Kylee called. "Dinner's ready."

"I'm going to April Tanner's house down the street," said Molly, poking her head into the kitchen but not crossing the threshold into what was still a disaster area. "She asked me over to dinner."

"What?" said Kylee. "You didn't tell me this?"

"You wanted me to start making friends. I made a friend. She invited me to dinner."

"You remember the Tanners?" said Ron. "Jessie, the track star was their son. April is Jessie's daughter. She's a good kid."

"See," said Molly. But her smile was too broad, her eyes too filled with sparkles as she looked from Ron to Kylee. "I'm just down the street and I'll be back before bedtime."

Before Kylee could think of a protest, her little girl turned on her heel. She was out the door just as Kylee regained her wits. Kylee turned back to Ron who was moving the take-out to the living room and out of the danger zone.

"I think my kid is trying to set us up," Kylee said trailing him.

Her back was to Ron as she spoke. She expected him to chuckle. Or to shoot down the idea. Or maybe, possibly, to confirm it might be something worth considering.

Ron said nothing.

Kylee sat in the corner of the sofa. It was the same couch from their youth. Though the television was no longer a box. Her dad had upgraded to a flat screen at some point in the last decade.

"Ron? Did you hear what I said?"

"About Molly? Yeah."

"It's ridiculous… isn't it?"

Ron shrugged. "It's actually quite common."

What was that Mr. Hot Commodity? Was this some new conceited side of her old bestie? Or had the smoke gone to Ron's head?

"Kids often do that with an authority figure," he continued. "She'll come to terms with us just being friends soon."

He sat down in the center of the couch, which had always been his spot. Ron turned to her, offering her a smile and some chopsticks. Familiarity and duck sauce washed over the mild attraction she thought she'd been feeling.

"Thanks, Ron."

"Anytime. That's what friends are for."

CHAPTER TEN

"Ouch."

"You okay?" Kylee looked up from her chicken and fried rice.

"Yeah," said Ron. "Just bit my tongue." Again.

It was the third time he'd bitten his tongue since they'd sat down to eat. He couldn't believe what he'd said to her before they'd dug into the take out. How had he let his big mouth tell the woman of his dreams that he wasn't interested in dating her? It was a lie and so his mouth was obviously attacking him to force out the words he truly wanted to say.

Kylee, I've loved you since the third grade.

Kylee, I should've come after you when you ran off with that jerk.

Kylee, I want to kiss you now and never let you go.

But he couldn't say any of that. Not because it was against the rules, but because of the perception. Ron had looked through the rule books. He'd spent the afternoon pouring over administration policy and procedures, and he'd found nothing.

There was no specific rule about teachers or administrators dating a parent. It was definitely frowned upon because of the liability issues and, again, the perception issue. Earlier today, Kylee had thrown on top of that pile, favoritism. Or could it be nepotism since they'd been like family most of their lives? Was there a word for showing preferential treatment to the woman you were in love with? Whatever the word, Ron knew he'd be called on it and any perceived advantage he might give Kylee could negatively affect his job.

What a mess.

Ron had taken a look at Thrive Learning Systems after the faculty meeting. Not because he had been cyberstalking Kylee. It was research for the good of the school. What he'd found just on the website had piqued his interest in the company.

He'd considered reaching out to them on his own. But now that Kylee was a part of the deal, and she had personally asked him for his consideration, he was firmly in Thrive's corner. She didn't have to give her presentation to ensure she had his vote. The woman already had his heart.

"Moo Shu?"

"Beg your pardon?" Ron looked up to see Kylee offering him some of the dish. "No, thanks, I'm full."

She snorted as she dropped the piece of food back in its carton. "I don't think I've ever heard those words come out of your mouth."

"I've gotta keep fit." Ron patted his firm stomach.

"Right, Mr. Hot Commodity. For all those hopeful moms."

Ron chewed at his lower lip, but the words came out anyway. "I'm not dating anyone right now."

"Me either."

They stared at each other for a second. Ron opened his mouth to speak then closed it. Kylee opened her mouth and then closed it. They both turned back to their plates.

Ron grabbed the morsel from the cartoon and shoved it in his mouth. He needed something to keep him quiet or he'd suggest a solution to their dating problem.

"Why aren't you dating?" Kylee said. "Are you

coming out of a long, tormented relationship that made you doubt your faith in the opposite sex, too?"

There was a self-deprecating smile on her lips. But it wavered when her glance met his. Ron had trouble swallowing past the lump that formed in his throat.

"Ky? Did he..?"

"Did Jason what?"

Ron couldn't form the words. He took in a deep breath. Then he clenched his fists. Just the mere thought of any harm coming to this beautiful, precious woman had him seeing red.

"Did Jason beat me? God, no. Emotional abuse, sure. Infidelity, probably more than I know about. But no, he never raised his hand to me or Molly. He wasn't around enough to even consider it."

Ron held her gaze. There was so much pain there. Guilt washed over him. "I'm sorry, Ky."

"What are you sorry for? You didn't marry him."

"No, but I should've stopped you from marrying him."

"Ron, that's ridiculous. My mind was made up." She crossed her arms over herself and leaned away slightly, as though protecting herself from the memory. "I was wrong, of course. But there was nothing you could've said to change my mind back then. I thought I had all the answers."

Ron placed his arm along the back of the couch. It wasn't an embrace, but it was the closest he could come to it. "I should've kidnapped you or something."

Kylee threw her head back and laughed.

"What's so funny? I could've done it."

"Whatever." She clucked her tongue. "You were skin and bones back then. Barely a hundred pounds."

"What? I wouldn't have been able to physically accost you? Are you saying you could've taken me."

"I could take you now." She gave him a playful shove.

"In your dreams, Bauer." He shoved back.

Kylee gasped, as though affronted. But her eyes sparkled as she did so. "Oh, it's on, Kidd. You want some of this."

She rose to her knees on the couch and shoved at his shoulders. Ron easily deflected her jabs. He landed some playful taps of his own on her shoulders and forearms.

"Woman, do you see these muscles?" He got a jab into her belly that had her double over with laughter. "They weigh a hundred pounds each."

"No, that's your ego giving off all that weight."

She straightened and gave him another punch. She'd put a little more momentum behind it and she fell forward. Ron caught her in his lap.

His arms came well and truly around her this time. She was cradled in his lap as though she were a damsel and he'd just lifted her from danger into the safety of his hold. Her head tilted back as she gazed up at him.

They'd play fought like this before. As kids. They were grown now. Kylee was all grown woman with curves and humps and bumps. And holy heaven did she smell good with the sweetness of duck sauce and the tang of soy sauce coming from the long sigh that escaped her lips. Could that be the smoke from the kitchen fire going to his head?

No. It was Ron's long-held, tightly pent-up desire for the woman he currently held in his arms. She felt so right here.

"Ouch." Kylee grimaced.

"What's wrong?"

"I think my hair is stuck to something."

Ron lifted the arm cradling her only to find his metallic watchband had caught in her tresses. "Hold still."

Ron slowly worked the strands of her hair out of

the links of his watch. The maneuver brought their heads closer together. He felt her breath on his cheek. He ached to taste the sweetness of her lower lip. With her hair free, Ron set his watch on the coffee table.

Kylee shifted and Ron helped her up. She took her time righting herself. Ron took his time relinquishing his hold on her.

They sat side-by-side in silence for a moment. Their cartons were empty. But the air was filled with palpable energy.

"If I had it all to do again," he said. "I would've used all my strength to lock you away until you realized that you deserved better than him."

Kylee gave him a small smile, but sadness pulled at the corner of her eyes. "It's in the past."

"Yes, it is. This is the present. I was weak then."

"And, what?" Her smile broadened. "Now you're strong. Those are the lyrics to a song."

"Yes, I am. I am strong now."

Her smile faltered as she gazed at him. "And if I tried to date another jerk?"

"He'd have to get past me first."

Ron watched her swallow. Her lips were right there for the taking. She wasn't pulling away from him. No, she was leaning towards him. His dream was just an inch away from him. All he needed to do was reach out and take it.

It was happening. It was happening just like he'd dreamed of as a kid sitting on this very couch with her. It was happening just like he'd planned after she walked back into his life the other day and he'd begun daydreaming again. Funnily enough, his adult plans still had this scene taking place on this same couch.

They'd be eating take-out. He'd turn to her and tell her how he felt. Then she'd lean in and tell him she felt the same way. They'd get closer and closer until their lips met.

They were getting closer now. Her gaze had dipped to his mouth. It was all coming together… except for the wailing saxophone that suddenly blared from the other room. And had the lights just dimmed down low on their own?

Kylee shut her eyes and groaned. "It's Molly."

Kylee pulled away from Ron and stood. She went into the other room; the sunroom just off the kitchen which had been turned into a library complete with a stereo system. Ron saw Molly's coat on the office chair, but the girl was nowhere in sight. How long had she been back?

"I'm sorry." Kylee turned off the sappy sax music

with a flick of a button. "Like I said, Molly's decided I should date you. And, like I said, it's ridiculous."

Ron took a deep breath. Instead of holding back, he let his tongue run free and speak for his heart. "It's really not that ridiculous."

CHAPTER ELEVEN

"That's not any kind of a test question I've ever seen."

Kylee looked down at her pad of paper. Instead of the bubbles of multiple-choice questions or the straight lines of fill-in-the-blank answers, she'd drawn a series of hearts and pointy arrows. Ron's name was filled in on a couple of the arrow shafts.

She turned the paper over and looked up to address Anthony. His man bun looked particularly tight today. As usual, he wasn't looking at her. His gaze was glued to his handheld device.

Kylee wasn't sure if it was a phone or a tablet or something in between. It was larger than his palm. But she'd seen him hold it up to his ear and talk. His thumbs moved at a rapid clip as he spoke to her.

"I hear you landed a pitch meeting at Barton Elementary School."

"Yes," said Kylee, straightening her array of number two pencils. Her cell phone, an Android that was five years old, sat quietly next to the pencil holder on mute. "I know the principal there. He and I, we… We're…"

She didn't know what they were? Last night at dinner, Ron had opened a door she'd never known was there. A door where they could be more than friends. Kylee was curious to poke her head inside the crack of this just barely opened door and see where it might lead.

"You got the deal." Anthony tapped his thumb a number of times in one spot. Then he pressed his index finger down, paused, and swiped right. "Good for you. Now you just have to close it."

"Oh, there's no guarantee they'll choose us. Ron, I mean Principal Kidd, has always been very fair in things like this. He's the type of guy who'll weigh all the options and pick the best one regardless of personal feelings."

Anthony's fingers paused and he looked up. It was the first time Kylee had seen his eyes. They were a shocking shade of blue. That, with his dark hair, made him quite handsome. If he ever took the time to look a woman in her eyes, she'd likely fall hopelessly in love with the color alone.

"You call him Ron?" said Anthony.

"I... uh, yeah. We're... friends."

Friends seemed the safe word to Kylee. It was also the most-true word. They hadn't gone through the door from friends to... more. Ron had just put it out there. He hadn't pressed. That wasn't his way. She'd always admired that about him.

Ron was the best listener she knew. He was the most level-headed person she knew. He was the fairest, most balanced person she knew.

She'd known all these facts when they were kids and he'd urged her not to run off with Jason. He'd warned her that it would ruin her life. It was the one and only time they'd argued outside of a class assignment. Ron had made a level-headed assessment of the decision that Kylee was making and called foul.

Kylee wished he had rescued her back then. She felt she was floundering now. Except for these past few days he'd been back in her life. She felt grounded around him, like her old self.

"Work that angle."

Kyle blinked. Anthony's blue gaze came back into focus. "Angle?"

What was this angle people were constantly bringing up? She knew she worked for an education company, but somehow, she didn't think this had to do with math.

"The friendship angle," Jason said as though it were the most obvious thing in the world.

"I'm not going to use my friend to get ahead in my job."

That might happen in the capital, but here in Adalia people helped each other because it was the right thing to do. There were no angles in the small town. There were only straight lines that got people to the points they wanted to go and circles of unity to include all of the community.

"Close the deal and you could get put on the high-level testing team."

Kylee opened her mouth to protest louder but paused. There was that carrot again. The high-level testing team was where they worked on post-secondary materials. It was Kylee's dream to work on college prep tests.

That team was now walking into one of the conference room doors down the hall. The door closed behind them, shutting her out. But what if it opened for her?

She didn't need an angle to talk to Ron. She was

already in his circle of trust. They hadn't talked about Thrive last night because the whole door opening situation had distracted them both.

Kylee had seen the work of the other company, Here 2 Learn. Their lesson plans lacked detail. Their competencies were vague. And their test questions were confusing.

She knew her work was beyond what they did. On assessment alone, she ran laps around the other company. She didn't doubt she was the best woman for the job.

There would be no angles necessary. This would be a straight shot. She'd show that to Ron later, the next time he came to her door. Just the thought of Ron showing up at her home made Kylee feel warm and mushy.

Kylee shook herself out of it. She looked to tell Anthony her decision, but he was already walking away, his head back down on his device. Kylee flipped her sheet of paper back over. The hearts and arrows stared back at her.

The hearts looked like the bubbles of multiple-choice answers. The arrows looked like blanks ready to be filled. But did Kylee dare ask the question? Did she want to fully open the door to the possibility of her and her best friend becoming more?

CHAPTER TWELVE

"Hasta Luigi, baby," said a fourth grader as she carefully placed a paper crown on her head.

"No, it's pasta la vista, baby," said a fifth grader as his salsa smudged crown fell to the floor.

Ron chuckled at the children as he filled their paper plates with refried beans, rice, and melted cheese. It was Taco Night at Buster and Eden's diner. The owners had allowed the school to use their kitchen as a fundraiser to help restock the arts programs. The quesadillas were aimed to get new instruments for the band. The nachos would hopefully bring in enough to refill the paint and crayon supplies for the art classes. And the rice and beans just might offer some leftover cash to go to the next class play for costumes and sets.

"The saying is *hasta la vista*, baby," said Ron. "That means see you later, *niño* in Spanish."

The two kids frowned at him. That was the one thing about trying to joke with the younger crowd. They didn't always get a clever, multilingual, multi-generational joke.

"*Bueno*," Ron said. "Go find a table and eat your tacos."

The two kids moved through the packed restaurant and found their family and friends. Ron tightened the apron over his collared shirt, which was amazingly still spotless, and his dark slacks, which had narrowly escaped a queso splatter. Though he'd long removed the paper crown from his head as the thin cardboard had begun to wilt under the heat.

"You were always such a show off in Spanish class."

Ron couldn't hide his smile at the sound of her voice. "*Buenas tardes*, Señora Bauer."

"All I can remember is *me llama*, Kylee."

Kylee shook her head. Her own paper crown slid to the side, but didn't fall off. Instead it clung to her locks like it wanted desperately to hold onto them. Ron understood the sentiment.

He felt heat rise to his face as he gazed across the serving table at Kylee. He gave a tug to his collar. Though he'd already loosened his tie, he still found himself a bit breathless in her presence.

"Hi, Principal Kidd." Molly's voice was singsong. Her own paper crown sat securely on her head as though it knew the little lady was born for the role.

Molly's eyes twinkled as she looked between him and her mother. Ron noted that Kylee's cheeks were flushed too. Was it possible she was feeling the same heat for him that he was feeling for her?

They hadn't come to any consensus the other night when he'd opened the door to the possibility of them dating. After he made the suggestion, neither of them quite knew what to do next, especially not after Molly had tried her hand at DJing. Ron had left shortly after Kylee had turned the music off. As they'd stood on the stoop of her front porch, the possibilities had lingered between them.

They couldn't continue the conversation now, not with half the community passing in and out of the restaurant.

Ron piled white rice, pinto beans, and cheese on

Molly's plate, as per her request. When Kylee held out her plate, Ron didn't wait for instruction. He put soft shells on her plate, brown rice, black beans, and tons of cheese.

"This is exactly what I wanted," Kylee said bringing the plate up to her nose.

He knew it was. Because he knew her so well. They'd spent many a Friday night at Taco Bell working on college admissions essays and planning for their respective futures.

He took Kylee's plate from her and plopped down guacamole.

"Hey," she protested.

"You're a growing woman," he taunted, knowing she wasn't a fan of most green foods. "You need a vegetable."

"Avocados are a fruit. So are tomatoes."

She had him there. He hadn't really cared whether she was eating every food group. He just wanted to keep her company for a little while longer.

"Principal Kidd, you left your watch at our house when you were over last night," said Molly. The little girl's voice carried over the Top Forty tunes coming out of the ancient jukebox. A few glances turned their way.

Kylee's cheeks turned redder than the salsa on her plate. Ron was sure his did as well. This time he couldn't blame the burners. Kylee's gaze met his. Once again, they were the only two people in the room.

"I can drop it off tomorrow," said Kylee. "Or you can swing by later...?"

Kylee shrugged her shoulders as she let the sentence trail. Ron was mesmerized by that shrug; how her collarbone became more pronounced. One shoulder was higher than the other making an asymmetrical shape that he wanted to measure. By the curve of her lip and the way she looked up at him from beneath her lashes, she wanted him to fill in the blank she'd left.

Ron knew his answer, but before he could complete the request, there was the sound of a throat clearing, followed by the high-pitched voice of an irritated child.

"You're holding up the line," said Ricky, Jr.

Ron wasn't the only teacher manning the food station. There were three others. But of course, Iman Hilson would come to his line expecting special treatment.

"As I live and breathe," Iman drawled. "If it isn't Princess Kylee."

Kylee grit her teeth. Her family had lived in this town long enough that no one bothered with ceremony. His Royal Highness Prince Edvard Nicholai Bauer was simply Eddie when he'd walked the streets every evening. The only time the Bauer's royal status was brought up was when someone wanted to drag the family through the mud. Like when their little princess ran off with the town bad boy.

Seeing as that little dig didn't get a rise out of Kylee, Iman went for the jugular. "Did you return to your maiden name? Or are you still holding onto Jason's?"

Kylee had never done fake well. It was why she and Iman rarely crossed paths back in high school. Kylee had seen right through the mean girl's fake friendliness.

"Nope, it's Bauer. I smartened up and cut both the name and the man loose."

"Oh," Iman pressed her hand to her heart and her face contorted into a compassionate grimace that didn't reflect in her gaze. "I had heard Jason found someone else."

Kylee bobbed her head, the crown slipped down to her ear, holding on by a few strands of her lush hair. "He's probably found a few more someone else's by now. I'd be happy to be your reference if you want to wait in his line."

And with that, Kylee turned her back on Iman. But not before giving Ron a quick smile. "See ya?"

Ron couldn't articulate after that performance. He was too busy trying his hardest not to fist pump Kylee's retort. But he didn't need words with Kylee. He knew she saw clearly in his gaze that she would indeed see him later tonight. And tonight, he planned to say every flowery, romantic word he'd ever dreamed of saying to her.

Before Kylee stepped away from the serving table, Ron reached out and fixed the crown on her head, securing it back in its rightful place. Kylee gave him another warm smile. Then she and Molly headed off to find a table.

"My dad left a watch collection at my mom's house," Ricky, Jr. was saying. "You can come to my house and see it."

Ron took the kid's plate and began loading it up. "Why not bring it in for show and tell? With your mom's permission, of course?"

Ricky nodded as he took his tacos from Ron.

Ron began on Iman's plate. He moved as quickly as possible so that she could move on and take her false smiles with her and out of his line.

"Looks like you're showing interest in a parent," said Iman. "Isn't that against the rules?"

"But Mom, I want him to show interest in you," said her son.

"I always knew you had a thing for her," Iman said, ignoring her kid as usual.

Ron didn't respond. He simply handed the woman the lettuce and beans she'd indicated that she wanted.

"Well, you better not let it interfere with business," Iman said as she took her light fare in one hand. "You wouldn't want to be accused of showing favoritism to your girlfriend."

"Kylee's not my girlfriend. She's my friend."

But even Ron didn't believe his own lie. He could tell Iman didn't either. She walked off and took a seat with some other parents. By the glances they stole at Ron he was sure that his relationship status with Kylee was the topic of conversation.

He wasn't breaking any rules. However, before his eyes, people's perspective about him was changing. The question was, did he care?

CHAPTER THIRTEEN

Kylee fixed her skirt, giving the pleated hem a tug. It came above the knee. Was that too high? Or maybe it wasn't high enough?

She'd changed three times, showered, put on makeup, taken makeup off, and then reapplied. Not in that order. Looking in the mirror her cheeks looked more plum than blush. She was so nervous that she was going to break out in hives.

Why was she so nervous? It was just Ron; her old buddy, her old pal. He was just coming over to pick up his watch. They might sit and talk. And...

And? What and? There was no and. And that was that. Except there was still the door that he'd left open.

It's really not that ridiculous.

What exactly wasn't ridiculous? Molly wanting them to date? Or the possibility of Ron and Kylee dating? He'd never clarified.

Kylee hated vague statements. There was always a right and wrong answer. She'd never let such an open-ended question like that get by as one of her test questions. So the first thing she'd do when Ron stopped by was to ask him to clarify his meaning so that she'd best be able to narrow down her response.

"Looking good, Mom." Molly poked her head in the bathroom door. "Now, that's how you dress for a date."

"This is not a date." That had not been made clear. Yet.

It also wasn't an angle. She wouldn't use her friendship with Ron to get her anywhere. She'd been used enough in the last ten years by Jason. This was simply a reconnaissance mission. Ron would retrieve his watch and Kylee would then interrogate him.

"Are you wearing lip gloss?" asked Molly.

Kylee put a finger to her lips. She'd slipped on one coat of gloss. But only because she hadn't gotten enough water today and her lips were parched.

"Is that eyeshadow?"

The shade matched her blouse.

"And earrings?"

Well, they complimented the embroidery in her skirt.

"It's a date, Mom."

"It's Ron," Kylee protested. Her cheeks flamed even brighter accentuating the makeup she applied.

"I like Mr. Kidd."

Kylee sighed. "I like him too."

"He likes you. He's always staring at you and grinning."

"He does? Oh my God, this is a date."

Molly nodded.

Something bubbled up in Kylee's chest. Was that heartburn? Or excitement? Probably excitement since she'd eaten the tacos only a couple hours ago. Kylee was feeling excited about dating her best friend.

But wait. Did Ron think this was a date? He'd made that joke about being a hot commodity around moms. Did he think Kylee was trying to commoditize him? Was that even a word?

Oh, no. What if Ron thought that she thought that this was a date? Or worse, what if he thought the only reason she'd asked him over was to work an angle?

But there had been that moment between them the other night when their fingers had interlocked while they'd sat on the couch. And before that, back in his office when the air had positively sizzled between them. Hadn't it?

Kylee's man radar was off. It probably had never been on. Jason had swooped in unexpectedly while the system was preparing to turn on. Other than that, she hadn't seen interest in any other guy.

She was probably wrong. Or maybe she wasn't? She didn't know. She hated not knowing. But the one thing Kylee knew for sure was that her daughter wanted this to be a date.

Kylee turned to Molly who was still framed in the bathroom door admiring her mother's reflection. "Should we have a talk?"

"About what?"

"About... you know..."

Molly rolled her eyes and groaned. "We already did the birds and bees talk."

"No," said Kylee. "About what dating means? I just want you to know that if I start to date, it won't affect your relationship with your dad."

Molly kicked the toe of her tennis shoe at the

area on the floor where the wood of the hallway turned to the tile of the bathroom floor. "He missed our call last night."

"Maybe he was traveling?"

"You always make excuses for him. You don't need to do that anymore. I'm not a little kid."

"Oh, I beg to differ, missy." Kylee bent down to be on level with her daughter. She didn't have to bend as far anymore. Molly was getting so big. "You'll always be my baby."

"I'm not a baby," Molly grimaced. "And he's the adult. It's his responsibility to reach out to me."

The little woman was right. When had she become so grown up? Would her father ever be the grown-up that she needed? Kylee doubted it, but she did hope so. For Molly's sake.

The doorbell rang pulling Kylee's attention. Kylee straightened, tugging her skirt again as she did so.

"Your date is here," Molly grinned. Then she tilted her head back and gave an exaggerated yawn. "I'm feeling tired. I'm going to my room. I won't come down at all tonight."

The door to Molly's bedroom closed with a quiet snick. Kylee made her way down the steps. She fingered her earrings, wondering if they were too much. She touched her lips wishing she had a tissue to wipe off the gloss.

Before she knew it, she was at the front door. She knew if she opened it, whatever happened, there was no turning back. Her relationship with Ron would be different from that moment on.

She peeped through the hole. And there he was. His face was in profile as he looked up. The porch light illuminated the small smile on his face.

Kylee let her gaze rake over what she could see of him through the small hole. For the first time since he'd come back into her life, she allowed herself to simply look at him. She'd always made fun of the gray hair that shaded his young face. With a bit of age and wisdom in his countenance, it made him look devastatingly handsome. Ron looked capable, experienced, and it took her breath away.

Kylee gasped at the transformation that took place in her mind as her childhood friend turned into a very desirable-looking man. At that moment, Ron turned and looked right into the peephole. Had he heard her? Had he seen her? Had he caught her staring?

She expected him to push the doorbell again. But he didn't. Of course, he didn't. He was Ron. He waited patiently for her to show up.

Ron had always been patient with her. He'd always stood by and waited for her after school. He was always ready with a kind word or a joke if things didn't go the way she'd planned. She wished he'd been there for the last decade of her life.

Even if this wasn't a date, she knew she wanted this man back in her life. She wanted to spend as much time with him and his goodness as possible. She needed a light like Ron's to shine on her.

Kylee flicked the lock and turned the doorknob. She pulled it opened just a crack. Still hesitant at the change she knew was about to happen.

Ron's smile dazzled her from the other side of the door. "Hey."

"Hey."

His gaze dipped to her lips. She knew she no longer had to ask for clarity. This was definitely a date. She had to make a decision. It was now or never.

Kylee pulled the door wide open. "Come in."

CHAPTER FOURTEEN

The moment Ron stepped across the threshold into the Bauer foyer, he knew everything between he and Kylee had changed. His first clue? She had changed.

Of course, she'd changed in the metaphorical sense. That ten-year gap was still between them. There was so much about her life that he didn't know. But that wasn't the change he meant.

Kylee had changed her clothes. She'd gone from her buttoned-up office clothes to something a woman who wanted to impress a man without looking like she was trying too hard would wear. Her blouse wasn't low cut, but it showed off those collarbones that had mesmerized him earlier. The skirt she wore gave him a teasing display of her knees and just a hint of thigh. But most importantly, she was wearing makeup.

What woman coming home after a long day of work, and then stopping by for an after-school fundraiser, would return home at the very end of the day and make all these changes? A woman who wanted to impress a man.

Ron's heart did a flip and landed into his belly. Kylee Bauer had gone through all this effort to impress him.

Ron took the doorknob from Kylee's hand. He closed it behind him, with a quiet snick that reverberated through his entire being. His first steps were tentative, unsure. How often did a man actually walk straight into his dream?

He caught up with Kylee in two strides. The brush of her forearm against his sent a tingle down his spine. Ron gulped, trying to push down his desire. He had to keep repeating the maneuver because his craving for her wouldn't go away.

"Are you thirsty?" she asked.

"Yes. No. I'm fine."

They stopped at the couch. Ron waited for Kylee to sit. She slid her hand down her skirt and then, instead of going to the corner where she always sat, she took a place just off the center of the couch.

Ron folded himself down beside her. The sides of their knees brushed. He had to hold himself still as the tingles became electric sparks.

"Where's Molly?"

"She went to bed early."

"Oh."

Here they were again; alone on the couch. This was where the dream always turned, and she landed in his arms. What was hazy was exactly how he got her there in the dream world?

Kylee turned to him. She took a deep breath in through her nostrils, which raised her chest and exposed her collarbones. Ron's gaze caught and held on those twin peaks.

"Before I forget, here's your watch. And here's the pitch information from Thrive Learning Systems since I forgot to give it to you the last time."

Kylee handed him his watch and a packet. Ron took them and placed them on the coffee table.

"Ron?"

"Yeah, Kylee?" He tried to lift his gaze to hers. He didn't want her to think he was staring at her chest. He was, in a sense. Just not at the part of her chest that would normally get a guy into trouble for staring at.

"You're the best friend I've ever had."

Ron lifted his gaze to hers. Had he read this whole situation wrong? Was she about to friend zone him?

"I didn't realize how much I've missed you these last years until I saw you. Which sounds awful because it makes it seem as though I didn't think about you. Because I did. I thought about you a lot. And then I tried not to think about you. Because every time I thought about you, I'd come to realize how unlike you the man that I'd chosen to spend my life with was."

These were the words Ron had always dreamed of hearing coming out of Kylee's mouth. The problem was, he was having a hard time listening because he was so focused on the shine of her glossed lips.

"I don't want to lose you again."

"You won't," he said. "I've already told you; I'll kidnap you."

She tossed her head back and laughed, giving Ron the perfect view of her collarbones again.

"You're so funny," she said. "I forgot how nice it is just to hang out with you. And –"

"Ky?"

"Yes, Ron?"

"I'm going to kiss you."

He watched her response carefully. She didn't pull away from him. She didn't stand and demand he leave. She didn't shove him into the friend zone. Instead, she nodded.

"I suspected it might come to this," she said.

"You did?"

"Yes, there's something…" She waved her hand between their chests. "… between us."

"Yes," Ron grinned. "There is."

"So, I came prepared. I brushed my teeth and put on lip gloss."

"That was very considerate of you, Ace. I had gum on the way over."

"Smart," she nodded approvingly. "Because you had onions in your tacos? I flossed, too."

"Wow. You are way more prepared than me."

She made a tsking sound with her tongue. "I always was."

"Yeah," he agreed.

"Yeah," she parroted.

They were sitting just inches away from each other. The dream-Ron would've had her in his arms by now. The real-Ron was so focused on how to begin.

Should he reach for her? With which arm? His right arm which was on the back of the couch? Or maybe his left arm? But that would box her in, and he didn't want her to feel trapped. He wanted her to want him.

He decided to just go for it and leaned in.

Kylee blinked, as though she were coming to the realization that this was really about to happen. She took a deep breath and leaned in as well.

Within a half inch of her lips, Ron pulled back. "Isn't this strange?"

"Totally," she agreed, straightening to an upright position. "I mean it's me and you. Kylee and Ron. We're best friends and we're about to kiss. Who would have seen this coming?"

"Me. I saw it coming."

"Really?"

Ron nodded. "I've been dreaming about this for years."

"Years?"

"Since watching *Saved by the Bell* on Saturday mornings."

"I used to love that show."

"I know," he said. "When Zach kissed Kelly I realized I wanted to do the same to you."

"You had feelings for me all the way back then?"

"I've had feelings for you my whole life, Ky. When we were in elementary school, I knew I wanted to share all my snacks with you. When we were in middle school, I knew I wanted to kiss you. When we got to high school, I knew I wanted you to be my girlfriend."

"I didn't know. How didn't I know this about you? I know everything about you."

"I didn't want you to know. Until it was too late."

"It's not too late. You're right on time. Like always." Kylee shifted until the last remaining inch between them was gone. She was nearly in his lap again. This was where his dream always began.

"Are we gonna do this or what?" she said.

"Quit bossing me, woman."

"Then get to it already-"

Ron's lips met hers. He landed softly, his bottom lip gliding across the smooth surface of her glossed lips. It may have been a gentle attack, but the impact was explosive. They both held still, barely breathing as the touch of their lips rocked them to their core.

Ron's right hand left the back of the couch and cradled Kylee's head. His left arm came up and boxed her in, wrapping her up inside the cage of his heart where he knew he'd never let her go.

He was certain that time passed as they held each other, explored each other slowly, and shared each other's breath. But the only time Ron was aware of was the ten-year gulf that had been between them slowly recede away until they could reach each other again.

Yes, things had changed. They would continue to change. But the one thing that would remain the same was Ron's certainty that Kylee Bauer was the woman of his dreams. Now she would be his in reality.

CHAPTER FIFTEEN

Kylee couldn't stop pressing her fingers to her lips. Her top lip was swollen. Her bottom lip kept spreading wide into a grin.

She and Ron had spent the last few hours kissing. And then kissing some more. And then, for good measure, kissing a bit more.

He'd capture her bottom lip for a while and nibble on it. Kylee had let him, soaking in the sheer decadence of resting her head in the cradle of his palm while he explored her mouth. Then they'd break apart to catch their breath. They'd watch television. Inevitably, he'd turn and brush her lower lip, or she'd capture the side of his mouth, and it began all over again.

It had taken them three hours to watch the thirty-minute pilot episode of *Saved by the Bell: The College Years* because they had to keep rewinding to the place where they stopped watching and started kissing. It had taken another thirty minutes standing on the front stoop in the middle of the night saying goodbye.

At some point, one of the neighbors had flashed their porch lights at them like they were two randy teenagers. Ron had chuckled and pulled her closer. Kylee had giggled as she'd cuddled in the crook of his arms. She never wanted to leave his embrace, but eventually, he'd pulled away from her.

Ron looked different in the moonlight. He was the friend she'd turned to for most of her life. Now before her eyes, he'd transformed into the man she didn't want to say goodnight to.

Life was so wild. Just a week ago, Kylee had sworn off men. Now she couldn't wait to see where her relationship with Ron would go. The sun wouldn't rise fast enough for a new day where she could see him again.

The sound of the doorbell had Kylee sitting bolt upright in her bed. She shoved her feet into slippers to avoid the cold floor. The bell rang again, mirroring the pounding of her heart. He'd come back.

The sun wasn't anywhere close to rising. It seemed Ron was just as eager for their new life to begin as she was. She wasn't ready to take her relationship with Ron to the next level. They'd just gotten on the ground floor. But she wouldn't mind necking on the couch with him a little more.

Apparently, Ron was impatient to get back to it. He leaned on the doorbell letting it make an alarming sound that would wake up not only Molly but others in the neighborhood as well. It was very unlike him to be so impatient. But what did she know?

He'd changed so much over the years she'd been gone, but he was still very much the same. Except he didn't have slicked back, brown hair. And he'd never worn a leather jacket a day in his life.

Peeking through the peephole, Kylee saw that it wasn't Ron. It was Jason. He turned and those mischievous eyes glared at her through the one-way glass.

Kylee jerked her face back from the door. She folded her hands behind her back. She'd already opened a new door. She was happy with the scenery she found on the other side. She didn't want to go back through the dark past by opening a door to let her ex back in.

But Jason didn't let up on the buzzer. At this rate, he'd definitely wake Molly and the neighbors on the other side of town.

"What are you doing here?" Kylee demanded when she pulled the door open.

And there he was. Jason Romano. The bad boy on the bike who she'd road off into the sunset with and drove straight into a tornado. He was leaning against the doorframe, his dark hair falling into his dark eyes. Kylee had once gone gaga when he struck that pose. Now all she wanted to do was barf all over his leather jacket.

"About time," Jason grumbled as he pushed his way in. "Where's Molls?"

"Asleep. It's one in the morning."

Jason nodded. "I was hoping to see her. You know, spend some quality time. But if she's sleeping, I'll just wait until the morning."

"Fine," said Kylee, motioning to the open door. "You can wait wherever you're staying and come back for breakfast."

"But I'm already here. No sense in going back out in the middle of the night."

Kylee stared him down. A sick feeling settling

in her stomach where butterflies from kisses from Ron had just been. She knew where this was going.

"I just need to crash for a couple of nights," said Jason.

"Absolutely not."

"Mom?" came Molly's voice from the top of the stairs. "What's happening?"

"Hey, baby girl," said Jason.

Molly came down another rung of the staircase. She squinted in the dim light of the hall. "Dad?"

"Surprise." Jason held out his arms as though presenting himself like he was some great present.

Molly stared mutely.

"I came to see you." He made his way over to the steps and scooped her up and into his arms. "I missed you so much."

"I missed you, too." Molly's voice was still groggy from being pulled from her sleep so late at night. She found her mom. Then she looked to the couch, likely searching for Ron.

"Hey, I have an idea," Jason said as he put her back on her feet. "How about we have a sleepover like when you were five?"

"Ok. But I can't stay up. I have school in the morning."

Jason blew air through his lips at that idea. "You can blow off school for a day."

"No, she can't," said Kylee, still standing in front of the open door as though there was a chance she could still get her ex out of it. But she knew it was a lost cause.

"Well," said Jason. "I'll read you a bedtime story so you can fall back to sleep. How about that?"

"Sure, Dad."

Jason took to the steps. "See you in the morning, Kylee."

Kylee closed the door as she watched the two head up the stairs. Before the door closed, a cold gust of air blew in on what had earlier been a warm and sunny day.

CHAPTER SIXTEEN

Ron kept pressing his fingers to his lips. He was certain they were still swollen from gorging himself on Kylee's mouth last night. If people couldn't tell he'd spent part of the night making out with his new girlfriend, then he was certain they'd be able to tell by the huge grin on his face.

Kylee Bauer was his girlfriend. At last. No, they hadn't discussed labels. They'd been too busy wrapped up in each other's embrace and pretending to watch TV. But that's what they were.

From friends to kissers. After a prescribed amount of time, prescribed by Kylee since he was raring to go now, they'd move to husband and wife.

It was exactly the path Ron always dreamed his life would take. A path he'd walk with Kylee on his arm. And now he'd arrived.

"We need to make a final decision about the test prep company."

Mrs. Steen's voice cut through Ron's daydreaming like a butter knife that had slipped down the sink into a garbage disposal. Unfortunately, he couldn't flip a switch to stop the grinding sounds. And so, Ron reluctantly left his dream world and came back to the present.

It was an early morning teacher's meeting. His time was running out. He needed to make a decision on the test prep company by the end of the week. His mind was already made up, but it would look good to show that he'd at least thought about the other companies vying for the job.

"Why not go with what's tried and true," said Mrs. Simmons. "We've had a relationship with Here 2 Learn for a few years now."

"Records show they're not up to date with the latest testing models," said Mrs. Steen. "I've taken a look at Thrive Learning systems and have been really impressed with their innovations."

"I'm surprised, Martha." Mrs. Simmons turned

her full attention to Mrs. Steen. "You typically prefer to do things old school, as the kids like to say."

Mrs. Steen nodded. "This is a new generation and they respond to different methods. I think we shoot ourselves in the foot if we don't change with the times and update what's not working."

Ron couldn't agree with her more. Of course, he didn't tell her that. He'd let the staff argue it out knowing Mrs. Steen usually got her way in the end.

The small group continued the debate as Ron looked down at Thrive's pitch packet. The sample questions and language didn't have Kylee's name on them, but he knew it was her handiwork. The questions were formed in common sense language, not confusing verbiage that could be interpreted in different ways. That was his Kylee.

His Kylee. Man, did he like the sound of that.

"Principal Kidd? Ron?"

Ron looked up. All eyes were on him. Brows were raised and pencils twiddling as though they'd been waiting to get his attention for a few minutes now.

"The room is divided," said Mrs. Steen. "Where are you leaning? With Here 2 Learn or Thrive Learning Systems?"

Ron pursed his lips and drew his brows in as though he were thinking hard on this big decision. It was a big decision. He'd just already made up his mind.

"I think it's time for a change," said Ron.

"He's going with Thrive," said Mrs. Steen, a rare look of approval on her stern face.

"Of course, he is," said Mrs. Simmons. "He's dating one of the company's personnel who also happens to be a student's mother."

The teachers had been gathering their items to leave believing a decision had been made which rendered their services no longer necessary. Now pencils clattered down to the table. Papers stopped shuffling. All eyes, once again, turned to him.

Ron cleared his throat and stood. If he were going to make a stand, he was going to physically stand in his truth. "I'm going with Thrive because, as pointed out by at least half of you, Here 2 Learn has made mistakes that have cost this school and our students in the past. We all know the stakes of these standardized tests. It's a high price, not only for the students but our job security as well. I've seen in their pitch alone that Thrive has clearly demonstrated that they are aware and have protocols to address those issues. The lead preparer also happens to be a mother of a student and a Barton alumna."

"So is Iman Hilson who works at Here 2 Learn," said Mr. Stevens.

"True," said Ron. "But like I said, that company hasn't addressed the mistakes of the past. We can't afford to have them repeated yet again. And yes, I'm dating Kylee Bauer."

A collective murmur went around the room. In a group of adults, Ron felt like he was back in grade school at the response.

"I've known her all my life," he continued. "Some of you have too and you know she is thorough and detail oriented and does phenomenal work."

"Oh, Kylee Bauer?" said Mr. Stevens. "The daughter of old Prince Eddie, god rest his soul."

A number of the teachers frowned. They were new to the old neighborhood and didn't realize that there was royalty in their midst. The Bauers had never done anything to draw attention to themselves. Other than Mr. and Mrs. Bauer's scandalous marriage.

Though Ron had never seen anything

scandalous about Mrs. Bauer. She had seemed to him like most of the other moms in the neighborhood, baking cookies, growing flowers, and doting on her daughter. He knew what the rumors were, that she had had an affair with Prince Edvard while she was still married. But Kylee had told Ron the truth.

Marilee had been separated from her abusive ex for two years before she'd met Eddie. The two had fallen madly in love. When Eddie's parents made him choose between a life as a third son who had little to no duties, and a life with Marilee, there had been no contest.

The two had come to start a life in Adalia, and left all scandal behind. Or so they thought.

"Yes, I remember little princess Kylee," Mr. Stevens continued. "She ran off with the biker kid, what was his name?"

Of course that scandal would rear its ugly head now. For months all anyone in Adalia could talk about was how the class valedictorian ran off with the town n'er do well. But like her parents' scandal, that was in the past.

"She's divorced now," said Ron.

"She just moved back into her parents' home," said Mr. Stevens. "I saw Jason Romano's bike parked out front of the house this morning when I was coming in from getting the newspaper."

Ron's world stopped. The eyes were back on him. He no longer felt tall in his big stand. His legs gave out. And he sat down.

CHAPTER SEVENTEEN

The vibrations of the ringing phone chime didn't sit well with Kylee. It went for two, three, and now four rising digitized bell tones. After the fifth ring, his voicemail came on.

"Hey, Ron. It's Kylee. Again. I know I'm calling during school hours." She looked over at the clock on her desk which told her it was after 3 pm.

She'd started these calls the first thing in the morning. The first at 9 am when she assumed he might be at his desk and able to talk for a second. But she'd gotten to the fifth bell on that first call. Then again at lunch. And now again.

"Well, it's after school now," she said into the receiver. "But if you could find a moment to call, I really need to talk to you about something. Okay. Bye."

She clicked off. Ron hadn't called or texted all day. It was unlike him.

Back in high school, he was always responsive. She didn't think any of her calls to him had gotten past the second ring. He'd never left a text message unanswered for more than fifteen minutes. Another batch of clues that she'd missed that her best friend had had feelings for her.

She wouldn't miss any more clues. She wouldn't miss any more chances. And she would be sure to not keep any secrets. She needed to tell Ron that Jason was back in town. She just didn't want to leave a voicemail about her ex sleeping on her couch last night.

Kylee had left Jason there this morning, on that same couch that she and Ron had shared their first kiss. She'd been too tired to fight with her ex. It was easier to deal with Molly's Terrible Two Tantrums than to convince, cajole, or command Jason to do anything he didn't want to do.

Kylee knew what she had to do to get Jason moving. She had to figure out what he needed, what he was there for. It certainly wasn't to see her. She doubted it was to spend time with his daughter.

More than likely, Jason was out of money and needed more. He had not been the best provider during their marriage. Kylee had had to work many an odd job as she struggled to raise Molly, attend school part-time, and keep up a household with a big baby constantly plopped down in front of the television watching cartoons.

She really didn't have any extra money to loan to him and never get paid back. But if it would get him gone and off her couch so that she and Ron could occupy it again, then she'd stop by the bank before going home.

It was almost quitting time. Just another ninety minutes to go before she could walk out the doors, scoop Molly from the after-school program, and try to find Ron in the flesh. Maybe she could sneak out a few minutes early? Her work was done. All she was waiting on was to hear who the school system had chosen to lead their test prep program.

Kylee knew that she'd done her best work with the pitch packet for Thrive. Someone in the office had gotten their hands on Here 2 Learn's pitch packet. It was a sham, filled with vague questions, errors in the answers, and outdated material. If Kylee were just a parent and not a competitor, she'd be the first in line at the Board of Education if that company was picked to prepare her daughter for a major test.

She had every confidence that Ron would see that. There was no need for any angle. It was all very straightforward. Thrive was the clear choice for success for the kids. And when Thrive was chosen, Kylee would be moving on up in the office.

She'd have a place at the post-secondary prep table. She'd have a new boyfriend who was respected and who respected her. And she'd be able to give Molly the financial and family-life stability that she'd had when she grew up. It was all falling into place.

"I hear that Barton Elementary is leaning towards our company," said Anthony. His man bun was sloppily drooping down to his neck today. For once, his eyes were on her and not on his device. "Good work, Bauer."

"Thank you," she said, taking in his praise. "I worked really hard on the pitch and the assessment questions."

Anthony leaned forward, his brows pressed together as though whispering about a conspiracy. "From what I hear that elementary school principal was quite impressed by you, if you know what I mean."

Kylee crossed her arms over her chest and leaned back so that she was not included in this contrived plot. "Principal Kidd was impressed by my work."

"Sure. That's why he came over to your house twice in the last week. Way to use what was in your test bank." Anthony chuckled at his lame joke.

Before Kylee could set Anthony straight, his head was back down, eyes glued to his device. She wished it was professional to throw pencils at work. But it wasn't. And she was done with anything resembling a scandal.

Ron was the furthest from scandal that she could get.

Well... except if people thought she'd used him to get ahead in her job. Which she hadn't. Anthony might think it. Others in this office might think it. But all Kylee cared was that Ron would never think it. And Ron's opinion was all that mattered to her.

When Kylee turned back to her desk, she noted in her peripheral vision that there was someone standing beside her desk. The man was tall with a head of gray hair.

Great. Her boss had heard the whole exchange. But when she turned fully to address the man who could make or break her, she was met with a wall of Ron.

Her first instinct was to stand and throw her arms around him. But she stayed in her seat. Something in the set of his jaw told her she wouldn't find that warm, soft place she'd cuddled into last night.

"Hey," she said.

"Hey."

No warmth in his voice either. His bright eyes were clouded over. His arms crossed over his chest, causing his suit jacket to tug tight over his muscles.

"Is it true?" he asked.

Oh no. He knew about Jason. She wasn't sure how, but she was sure of it.

"Let me explain," Kylee began.

Ron closed his eyes and pinched the bridge of his nose. She remembered him doing that when he was met with a particularly tough problem that he couldn't work out. She stood then and took a step toward him. But he stepped back.

"You were just using me to get the account?" he said.

Kylee's advance halted. "Wait? What?"

"Am I so blind?" He squinted at her. "Have you changed so much?"

Kylee looked from Ron to her co-workers looking down at papers or at computer screens pretending they weren't paying attention to the scene playing out.

"You actually think I was using you to get points at work?" Kylee said. "You can't believe I'd do something like that?"

The tightness in his jaw loosened for just a second. But almost in the same instance, it stiffened again. "I wouldn't have believed you'd run off with Jason Romano a decade ago. Or that he'd spend the night with you after I left you the other night."

"No," Kylee held up her hands. "That is not what happened. He showed up out of nowhere, without calling."

"And you let him in, late at night?"

"He wasn't there for me. He claimed he wanted to see his daughter."

"But that's not true?"

People were starting to openly stare. As much as Kylee wanted to believe she didn't care what others thought of her, she had to admit that wasn't exactly true.

She was making a good decision by choosing Ron. The best decision of her life had been kissing him. She had never cared about a crown, or connections. But she had always cared about this man.

She wanted everyone to know that she'd picked him. But she also wanted everyone to know that he picked her. Please let him still pick her.

"Ron, can we just go somewhere and talk?"

Kylee reached out to him. But Ron pulled away from her. The look of hurt and betrayal on his face brought back a memory. It was of the day she'd decided to run away with Jason.

Ron had talked until he was blue in the face. He'd debated her logic, attacked her reasoning, he'd even drawn a chart. But Kylee wouldn't be dissuaded. Again, she hadn't cared about any scandal her choice might led to. She'd been in love. Or so she'd thought.

When Kylee had walked away, this was exactly how Ron had looked at her. His eyes had been slits, as though it hurt to look at her. His mouth had been turned down in a frown of utter disbelief. And his shoulders had hunched in defeat.

Kylee hadn't thought about that moment again for nearly a year after she'd left. It had taken that long to realize that her best friend had been right. But she'd been too determined to make her relationship work. She'd tossed everything she had at the problem that was her marriage. But no single answer stuck until she'd decided to leave.

Ron had been right that day. He was wrong now. And now she had to make him see.

"Principal Kidd, we're so delighted to have you in our offices," said Syd Rowen.

Her boss approached the two of them with his hand out. Ron turned from Kylee and took the proffered hand.

"I hear you were impressed with Kylee's pitch."

"She made a very convincing argument." Ron didn't look at her as he spoke about her.

"She's a rising star here at Thrive. With the work she's done on the elementary school pitch, we're considering her for advancement."

"Well, it looks like we all have a decision to make," said Ron. "If you'll excuse me."

And with that, he turned and walked out, closing the Thrive office door behind him.

CHAPTER EIGHTEEN

"Principal Kidd, look."

Ricky, Jr. ran over from his classroom door to greet Ron in the hall. His hands yanked at the bright red tie around his neck. The kid could've been a mirror image of Ron as a young boy running through these halls with his white collared shirt, dark slacks, and ever-present tie.

"I tied my tie myself," the kid beamed up at Ron. "Well, my dad helped."

Ron gave the kid's tie an unnecessary straightening. It surprised him that Ricky, Sr. had stopped through town. The man traveled so much Ron only ever heard of him being around for the holidays. He'd always know that the elder Ricky had made a stopover or made time to call his son when

Ricky, Jr. was beaming bright smiles for the next few days.

"It must be nice to see your dad," said Ron.

"He's only here for a few days. Then he's back on the road. But we did play ball. Even though I'm not good at any sports. I taught him *Magic the Gathering*, but he wasn't very good. But he said we can play online tomorrow night when he gets to his hotel."

The kid ran off back to his class, beaming all the way. Ron had always had his father around every day of his life. Even after his parents divorced, his dad hadn't moved too far, just a couple of streets over.

When his mother remarried, Ron had the luxury of two dads who were both amazing. Poor Ricky, Jr. only got a half a dad. If only dads knew how important it was just to call their kids, to be a part of their lives any way possible.

Ron straightened preparing to head back to his office. He had the strongest urge to call his dad just then. When he turned, he saw Molly Romano watching him.

"Hey, Molly."

She didn't respond at first. She chewed her lip as she regarded him. Ron had watched her mother do that when they were younger. It had been Kylee's decision-making face. That was the face she made when she was chewing over whether an answer was correct, and she should mark it down.

"I don't agree," Molly finally said. "Sometimes dads don't make it better. Are you and my mom gonna break up now that my dad's around?"

When Molly had first shown up at Barton, she had been obviously trying to figure out how she would fit in. As a kid who hadn't had much permanence in her life, she'd likely figured she'd take on the role she was most used to; the role of the outcast.

In just a week, she'd found her place at Barton. Ron had seen her at lunch the other day sitting with a group of kids from her class, laughing and giggling like a little girl should. He hadn't heard a negative word out of Mrs. Steen about her. He'd peeked at Molly's latest grades and was thrilled to see that she'd received the highest marks.

Having found her place, having figured out where she fit, had had a dramatic effect on her life. And now something, or rather someone, from her past had come back to shake it up.

Ron walked over to the lockers Molly leaned against. He put his back to them and then tilted his head up and let out a sigh.

"She's been sad again since he came around," Molly continued. "She laughed and smiled and was happy when it was just the two of you. Me, too."

That warmed Ron's heart to hear, that he made Kylee smile and laugh and happy. He felt all those emotions when he was around her. He'd never felt so devastated at the moment he learned her ex was back in her life and he'd stayed over.

No. He had felt this devastation before. He'd felt it when she'd run off with Jason ten years ago, leaving him and everything they'd meant to each other in the dust of Jason's motorcycle exhaust.

"He never stays long," said Molly. "He'll probably leave after she gives him money."

Ron looked down at the little girl. Her little shoulders were weighted down as though the world sat there. "Come here, Molly."

There were rules about physical affection between kids and staff in an elementary school. But Ron didn't bother to heed the rules at this moment. He bent down and pulled the little girl in for a tight squeeze; a squeeze he hoped would ring all the worries from her adolescent body and knock that heavy weight from her back.

"Listen, Molly," he said, pulling away to look her

in the eyes, "Promise me something. Promise you'll let the adults deal with this."

"That's what my mom always says when my dad does something wrong. Which is a lot of the time."

"She's a smart lady, your mom. The smartest lady I know."

Molly searched Ron's gaze. After a moment, she nodded in agreement. He watched the little girl head into her class. She looked a bit lighter in her steps as she did so.

Back in his office, Ron looked down at the two pitch proposals on his desk. One company made repeated mistakes but managed to maintain a stellar reputation based on past connections. Another company was filled with innovators led by a person who'd made one mistake in her past.

Ron couldn't afford any more mistakes in the future of his school, his career, and these children. He knew what he had to do.

CHAPTER NINETEEN

Kylee was not having the best morning. Her eyes were crusted with dried tears. No makeup could fix the redness under her eyelids. Her skirt had threads dangling from a loose hem. She spilled mascara down the front of her shirt. Her phone was dead after checking it all night long. When she'd plugged it in this morning and gotten a cell of energy, she saw she still had no new messages.

"You okay, Mommy?"

"Oh, yeah, baby." Kylee sounded exhausted even to her own ears. "I'll get out of your way so you can get ready for school."

As Kylee made to step out of the bathroom door, she found herself stepping into her daughter's embrace. Molly wrapped her arms around her mother's waist and gave her a tight squeeze. It was tight enough to pull a few more tears from Kylee's dry eyes.

"I know that's not true," Molly said as she looked up at her mom. "I know you're not okay right now. But you're a smart lady. Mr. Kidd said you're the smartest lady he knows."

"He did? When did he say that?" Kylee sniffed. "He was talking about me? What else did he say?"

"He also said for me to stay out of it and let the adults handle it."

Of course, Ron would say that to a kid. For the last week, he'd been the best parent Molly had ever had. Kylee knew Ron would never turn his back on her daughter. She just hoped Ron would allow her back into his life as well.

"I just want to say that I love Daddy…but Daddy doesn't make either of us happy. Mr. Kidd does."

It was a struggle to not mess up her mascara with tears. Kylee pulled her daughter to her again. Even firmer this time. It took a long while before Kylee released Molly to take her place in the bathroom.

Coming down the stairs was like stepping into a war zone. Clothes were strewn around. Half eaten take-out food was spilling out of containers and onto the coffee table. Jason was asleep in front of the television, which was turned on at full blast, and he was in his boxers.

This was why she'd gotten divorced. The youngest person in the house was the most grown of the three. Kylee was putting a stop to this now. There was money burning a hole in her purse. But she didn't pull it out.

"Jason, get up." Kylee kicked at the base of the couch. She was very proud that she didn't kick his bare foot that was dangling off the cushions.

"It's seven in the morning." He groaned and turned over.

"Exactly. It's time for you to get up and get out of here. You are not my responsibility anymore. Do you hear me?" She gave another firm kick to the base of the couch, just narrowly missing his toes.

Jason looked up at her frowning. "Fine, I'll go. Just loan me some cash."

"Nope. Not gonna happen. The money I make is for me and Molly."

He sat up now, complete indignation in his face as though she'd just taken his favorite toy away. "What am I supposed to do?"

"You need to get yourself together. Or not. Your success or failure is on you. Not me."

"Fine. I'll be out of here tonight."

"No. Now."

Sixty minutes later, Kylee turned off the exit that would take her to work. Now that Jason's motorcycle tail lights were headed south, she could set everything on track again.

She was running late to work. But it was going to be her last day on the job. So, it didn't really matter.

She couldn't stay after the scene yesterday. As she walked into the office, she noticed people staring at her from beneath their lashes. A few gaped openly. She heard the whispers that included her name. And, of course, some spoke at full volume.

Kylee marched right up to Syd Rowen's office. Before knocking on his door, she turned and faced the crowd. She was not surprised to find they all were staring openly behind her back.

"For what it's worth," she began, "I didn't date Ron Kidd to get ahead. I didn't want to date anyone at all. But when a man like him, who is so incredible, comes into your life - back into your life, and he checks all your boxes and fills in every one of you blanks, you'd be stupid not to grab hold with both hands and pencil him into your life forever. And if I am lucky enough for him to give me a retake, that's what I'm going to do."

With her speech done, Kylee turned back to her boss' office to find the door open and Mr. Rowen staring down at her. Kylee handed him the letter she'd prepared last night.

"What's this?" Mr. Rowen asked.

"My letter of resignation. We lost the Barton account because of me. I take full responsibility for my actions."

"As you should. We won the account and I was told it was a direct result of your work."

"Mine? Me?"

"Seems the lessons you presented, the questions you crafted, and the process you created was the best. It looks like you were able to find the angle the teachers were looking for."

"The angle?" Kylee asked.

Mr. Rowen nodded, pride in his eyes. "We've been asked to give a presentation to the whole school this afternoon. Get ready. We're going to be late. When we get back, we'll talk about your future here."

Mr. Rowen took the letter from her and tore it into bits. Behind her, a slow, gulf clap broke out. It got louder and louder.

Kylee turned to see the appreciative gazes of her coworkers. Not one person looked at her as though there was a scarlet letter on her chest. The whispers continued, but Kylee picked out words like *she's lucky, she's smart*. Not a hint of scandal was uttered. But there was only one thing that rang through her ears.

Ron. Ron had chosen her. Did this mean there was a chance for them?

CHAPTER TWENTY

Ron pulled a whiteboard onto the stage in preparation for the school assembly. On one side of the board there hung a tacked-on banner that read "Welcome Thrive Learning Systems."

"I have to admit, this plan, these materials, look good," said Mrs. Steen as she looked over the more extensive packet that Thrive Learning Systems had delivered this morning. "I think your little girlfriend is just what we need to succeed on the standardized tests."

Ron didn't open his mouth to correct her. He hoped it wasn't too late to stamp that label on Kylee. He'd opted to make her test prep system an integral part of the school. It was a no-brainer. Her methods were the best option. For his heart, she was the only option. He just needed to let her know that.

He'd have his chance today. Thrive should be here any moment to give a presentation to the assembled school. Ron knew he couldn't talk to Kylee before the presentation. He had a plan that wouldn't require him to wait much longer after she was done.

It was nearly show time. Everything was in place on stage. The students were filing into the auditorium and taking their seats. All that was needed was the woman of the hour.

Ron didn't see her enter the auditorium. But he knew the moment she stepped onto the stage. The air changed and became electric. His pulse sped up ahead of his heart. His palms itched to be full of her. But he waited. He had a plan.

Syd Rowen took the stage coming to stand in front of the whiteboard Ron had pulled behind the podium. The youthful-looking gray-haired man could've stood in for Ron's older brother. "Thank you for having us."

The man launched into an age-appropriate speech about his taking tests in his youth. His antics and animated delivery had the kids giggling and actually listening. Rowen clearly understood his audience, and Ron felt even more certain that he'd made the right decision to put all his eggs in the Thrive basket.

As Rowen went on, he lost Ron's attention. Ron turned to a figure just off the stage, standing behind the curtain. Kylee was looking down at her notes. Ron knew from their youth that she didn't like speaking off the cuff. He knew she'd have her remarks prepared, not leaving anything to chance. That was his Kylee.

His Kylee.

When her gaze lifted, it found his immediately. He knew that, even through the crowded room, she'd seen him because she took a deep inhale. Ron watched as her shoulders rose. The movement accentuated her collarbones and Ron's mouth watered.

He hoped their silent communication was working today. He squinted his eyes, trying to let her know that he was sorry for his actions in her office. He'd been out of line and inappropriate to bring personal matters into a professional environment.

Kylee tilted her head to the side. In his heart, Ron was certain the movement was meant to tell him that he was forgiven, and also to ask for his apology for the debacle with her ex.

Ron nodded, eager to let her know that her apology wasn't needed. He needed Kylee to know that there was a blank space in his life, and she was the only answer to that particular question. He was certain she got his answer when she smiled back at him.

At this point, Ron was tired of the muted gulf between them. He wanted to use words, he wanted to use his hands, he wanted to use his lips. But there was a room of children between them, and Kylee was now being called to the podium.

Her boss said her name. When she didn't respond, because all of her focus was on Ron, Rowen repeated her name again. Kylee tore her gaze away from Ron and stepped up to the podium.

"It's all right to make mistakes," she said, not looking at her notes. "It's how we learn. A test should teach you something. That's the way I've designed these lessons for you guys. Would you like to see?"

The children gave a rousing chorus of agreement. Kylee turned to the whiteboard behind her. Instead of untacking the welcome sign, she turned the board around to the blank side. A chorus of giggles rose up at what was on the board.

Ron + Kylee = Forever was written in colorful dry erase marker.

Ron caught a few adult gazes go to Molly. Though the little girl had been a mischief maker in her first few weeks here, the kid's gaze was all innocence. Ron could attest that this time it wasn't her fault.

"Try the eraser," Ron called out as he walked toward the stage.

Kylee did. But instead of erasing the equation, the eraser put purple sparkles over the solved problem. Finally, Kylee put the eraser down and simply gazed at the writing on the board.

"I think this is permanent marker," said Kylee as Ron joined her on stage. Her voice carried in the microphone she still held in one hand.

"It is permanent," said Ron. "And you just sprinkled it with fairy dust which seals the deal."

Kylee's lips parted, but no words left her mouth. A single tear left her right eyelid and Ron caught it with his thumb. She blinked, looking up at him as though he were the answer to a problem that had challenged her for a while.

"Did I get the math right?" Ron asked.

"Yes," Kylee nodded. "You got the correct answer."

"I'd kiss you now, but we have an audience full of impressionable kids."

"It's a lesson they need to learn," shouted Mr. Rowen from the side of the stage. Beside him, Mrs. Steen dabbed at her eyes and shrugged, as though giving them permission.

Their encouragement was joined by the kids in the audience. For the first time in his life, Ron bowed to peer pressure and kissed the woman he planned to spend the rest of his life with in front of everyone that mattered to him. The sigh Kylee made against his lips was the bonus that told him he'd aced this final exam.

EPILOGUE

Molly grinned as she stared up at her mom and her soon to be step-dad. On their way out of the school auditorium, the kids had applauded, giggled, ew'd and ah'd as her mom and Principal Kidd pressed their lips together.

Molly hadn't applauded. She'd sat back with her arms crossed over her chest. A self-satisfied grin spread across her face at her handiwork. The same smile spread across her face as she sat across from the two lovebirds in the booth.

Principal Kidd placed a paper crown on her mom's head. He spent a few moments adjusting it to make sure it sat just so. Then he bent his head and kissed her again. If this were a cartoon, Molly was sure there would be blue birds and red hearts floating between them.

"Wow," Molly said. "That wasn't as hard as I thought it would be."

"What do you mean?" said her mother without looking at her

"Nothing," Molly said as she straighten the crown on her own head, then dug into the taco on her plate.

A bell chimed over the door of Buster and Eden's. There had been tons of chatter in the place in the late afternoon. Now it went silent. Everyone's gazes were on the couple framing the doorway.

"Didn't I tell you I'd take you places, my darling baker." A tall, dark haired man wrapped an arm around a blonde woman. The blonde appeared to pay the man no mind. Her gaze was on the taco bar. "They say this place has the best tacos in the entire kingdom. But I'll let you be the judge of that, Jan dear."

Molly crunched on her taco as she watched Ms. Eden make her way from the back of the restaurant to the couple. The older woman beamed as she bent into an awkward curtsey. That's when Molly recognized the man.

"Prince Alexander, what an honor."

"No, none of that," said the prince. "We're here to be served like any of your customers."

The blonde beside him rolled her eyes as the two followed Ms. Eden to the booth next to Molly's. As he sat, the prince looked over at her.

"That looks delicious," he said, eyeing her taco.

Molly knew better than to speak with her mouth full, so she gave the prince an enthusiastic nod.

The prince chuckled as salsa dribbled down Molly's chin. Then his focus went to Molly's mom. His gaze narrowed as he did so. "You look familiar."

Kylee averted her gaze and shrugged.

Molly, who had finished her bite, decided to answer. "I think we're cousins?"

The prince looked between the two. When his gaze slid back to Kylee, his eyes sparkled. "I see it now. You're my cousin Edvard's daughter."

"You knew my dad?"

"Not the man, but his deeds," Prince Alex grinned, his gaze traveling back to the blonde across from him. "He was the first of us to marry... out of line, as it were."

The blonde woman blushed. Maybe it was the reddening of her cheeks that made Molly recognize her. She was Jan Peppers. The American pie maker who was the best friend of Queen Esme. Both King

Leo or Prince Alex had married American girls. The four of them were always smiling in photographs and video. They looked nothing like the royals in the history books with scowls on their faces.

"And is this your Prince Charming?" asked Prince Alex, his gaze now on Principal Kidd.

"Even better," said Molly. "He's the principal, and he's going to be my new dad."

ABOUT THE AUTHOR

Shanae Johnson was raised by Saturday Morning cartoons and After School Specials. She still doesn't understand why there isn't a life lesson that ties the issues of the day together just before bedtime. While she's still waiting for the meaning of it all, she writes stories to try and figure it all out. Her books are wholesome and sweet, but her heroes are hot and heroines are full of sass!

And by the way, the E elongates the A. So it's pronounced Shan-aaaaaaaa. Perfect for a hero to call out across the moors, or up to a balcony, or to blare outside her window on a boombox. If you hear him calling her name, please send him her way!

You can sign up for Shanae's Reader Group at http://bit.ly/ShanaeJohnsonReaders

ALSO BY SHANAE JOHNSON

The Rebel Royals series

The King and the Kindergarten Teacher

The Prince and the Pie Maker

The Duke and the DJ

The Marquis and the Magician's Assistant

The Princess and the Principal

www.ingramcontent.com/pod-product-compliance
Lightning Source LLC
LaVergne TN
LVHW012107070526
838202LV00056B/5655